His Queen

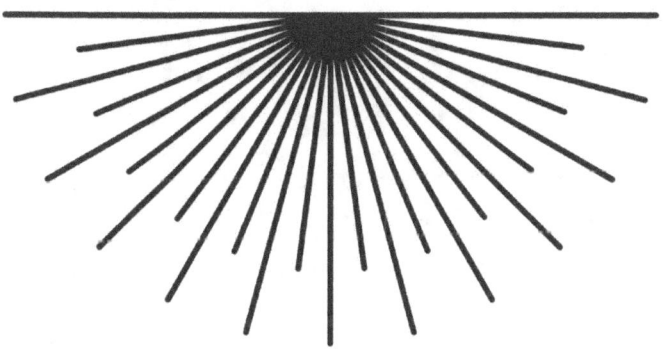

A 1920s Mafia Romance

J.C. Donovan

CONTENTS

To those who dream of a different time...

a different place...

a different life...

CHAPTER 1

Adelaide Sanna

1921

Auntie Ellen told me to dress in my best for Chicago. Black would be the most proper for the situation, she's said to me while giving me her Sunday best pearls to wear. Since she'd never steered me wrong before, so that is exactly what I did, and that is how I found myself on the train on Wednesday, dressed in a simple black dress, on my way to Chicago. It was my second trip to the city this year. I had gone in January to my mother's funeral, now I went to bury my father and brother.

I was officially an orphan... not that I'd known my parents at all. I'd been raised by Auntie Ellen and Uncle David since I was four. They lived in central Illinois on a lovely farm, where they had chickens, cows, and goats. They'd sent me to a small, one-room schoolhouse with their own children until I was fourteen. I'd nannied for two years for the mayor after that and helped on the farm.

Meanwhile, my parents and brother lived and worked in Chicago. They had a large house in the city with no animals. Not even a dog. My brother has private tutors. He'd worked in the family business.

The train began to halt, the wheel screeching against the tracks as we cruised into Central Station. I did not know who would receive me at the station, but I knew the kind of man I'd be looking for in the crowd. I grabbed my bag and got off the train, looking for my name amongst the crowds of people waiting in the grand hall. It isn't needed, though, I recognized the man waiting for me. My cousin, Cristiano. When I approached him, he gave me a small hug and a sympathetic gaze.

"I'm sorry for your loss, Addy," he greeted me. "I've taken care of the many preparations for the service. Nonno is beside himself with grief."

"I'm sure," is all I can reply as he leads me to his car. Rather, what I recognize as my father's car. His 1917 Ford sat in wait for us. Cristiano opened my passenger door before climbing into his driver's seat.

"I'll take you home first, then we can go to the church so we can go over the Sunday service," he explained to me as we began our short drive to my family's home in Gold Coast. Cristiano kept speaking during the drive, talking to me about all the nice things he's done for my father and brother since their death. Including reminding me of all he did for Mother's funeral as well.

"It must be hard, being back home since you lost your mother in January."

"Cristiano, I never knew them," I finally said. It wasn't anything he didn't already know. He and Angelo were the same age, ten years older than me. He knew I had been sent away to live with my mother's sister downstate, and I'd only been to Chicago four times in my life. Today is the fifth. Yet, he expected me to play a grieving daughter and sister, the way I had in January when my mother died. Everyone expected me to love them because they are my blood, but no tears would be shed for them. I didn't know them or love them.

At the family's home, a maid came out to take my bag from me before I entered the house. Two large men stood outside the home, most likely standing vigil for my father and waiting for my return. I nodded to them both as I entered the white stone building. Nonno sat in his wheelchair in the parlor. He hasn't walked in nearly ten years, and Angelo told me in January that the next time I'd be in Chicago would be for his funeral. He was wrong, Angelo usually was when it came to me.

"*Nipote, sei tu?*" Nonno asked as I entered the parlor and knelt beside him. In recent years, English has slipped his mind, and all that is left was the Italian from his home country. Neither Auntie Ellen nor Uncle David spoke Italian, but the Father of our local parish did, and they sent me to church twice a week to learn from him. They said it was important I learn my family's native language.

"Hello, Nonno," I greeted him, placing my hand on his leg. "Are you well?"

"*Dov'è tuo padre? Vorrà vederti.*" He asks for my father, his eldest son and the only one of his children still living until four days ago. It was a dangerous business that my family kept. Running the underground for the Italian Mafia. My Nonno grew the business sixty years ago when he came to the United States. Before settling in Chicago, he worked for the Italian Mafia in his home country. When he got old enough and married my nonna, they decided to move and start their own operations here in the States. What started as a bar on the south side grew to multiple lounges and restaurants that were fronts for the Chicago drug trade and money laundering. When prohibition began two years ago, my parents entered the alcohol scene as well. Selling beers, Italian wines, and southern-made whiskeys in addition to their drug trade. Angelo was already managing most of the longues when he died, my parents' involvement turning minimal with their age.

The business killed them. After Mother died of influenza in January, Father decided to grow the drug trade again, pushing more product than he had in previous years. Four days ago, while they were both inspecting the newest shipment, police cornered them, and a gunfight ensued. Both my brother and father were shot and died later from those injuries in this very house. Seven others died as well, either on the scene or later due to gunshot wounds. According to public records, my father died of cardiac insufficiency, and my brother of a gardening accident in the backyard after hearing of my father's death. Cristiano had covered it up well.

I turn to Cristiano, "Does he not know?"

"We have told him three times. Nonno is old, Addy, he forgets often," my cousin explained to me. I stood then with a sigh, kissing my grandfather's cheek. "I've been staying here with him since their death."

Another favor he no doubt plans to check in as soon as the lawyer comes to see us and reads the will. No doubt I'll have a nice inheritance, but I'm sure their business will go to Cristiano. Judging by the two men outside, I'm sure all my father's men already consider my cousin the new boss in town. I'm sure everyone in Chicago knows he's the new head of our branch of the mafia. Soon, the news will reach New York, where the American head of the mafia lives, and when he hears it, it will all be official.

"You can return home tonight, I can stay with Nonno," I told him. "Thank you."

"I can stay, Addy," he insisted. "Make sure you both are okay."

"We will both be okay." I didn't want him to stay. Cristiano worked like many mafia men; it was all favors for them. He would take care of me, of that I am sure, but it would cost me eventually. It would cost me something to continue letting him help me. Probably my future, after all, I am Luciano Sanna's daughter and Lucilio Sanna's granddaughter, Cristiano, as one of my closest male relatives, could insist on a high-profile mafia wedding, to improve his position. Sell me back to our homeland to gain a connection back home in *Italia*; or set me up with one of the families that run the other cities. The Tosellis in San Francisco; the D'Agostinos in New Orleans; the Adessos in Detroit. Any of their sons would be seen as suitable matches for me.

"Alright, I'll leave Bruno and Felix outside if you need anything, just ask them," Cristano reminded me before leading me to my home. Technically, the family home still belongs to Nonno, but my parents lived here with Angelo until their deaths. Father never lived anywhere else except this house.

"Nonno?" I knelt back down beside him. "Are you hungry?"

I cooked dinner, a classic puttanesca that I had learned years ago. I fed Nonno and got him ready for bed. I claimed one of the guest rooms for myself, never really having a room in this house. I must have had one when I was a baby, before I moved in with Auntie Ellen and Uncle David. Now, I just chose the guest room decorated with blue floral wallpaper and a powder blue quilted bed. I stayed in this room last time I was here.

I go through the house, going to lock the doors. Out front, Bruno and Felix sit on the front porch, smoking. I secure my dressing robe around my front before taking out two glasses of whiskey I found in a cupboard. I set down the glasses for the gentlemen.

"Thank you, Miss Sanna," Felix took his glass first, sipping the liquid.

"Was he a good man? A good boss?" I asked them quietly, knowing I should just go inside and go to bed. I didn't know my father, but these men did. I wanted to know what kind of man he was, and the only way I'd know now is through the men who worked for him.

"Your father was the best boss," Felix told me, offering a kind smile. "He wanted the best for your brother and you."

"And Cristiano, will he be a good boss? Good to the Sanna name?"

They both sit quietly, digesting my question. Bruno takes his time with his whiskey. I stand there, swaying back and forth as I wait for an answer. When I don't think it's coming, I turn around. They won't talk mafia business with me. I may be Luciano Sanna's daughter, but I'm his *daughter* and not his son. Not his heir.

"Miss Sanna," Bruno called after me as I started up the stoop. I turned, giving him my full attention. "No."

I gave him a single nod in response before

going back into my house. He's not my father, nor is he, my brother. These men know that, and now so do I.

CHAPTER 2

Adelaide Sanna

A full catholic mass was performed that Sunday for my father and brother's funeral. Afterward, we all gathered at the cemetery to have them buried. Father next to mother and Angelo to their right. Every mafia man in the city and some from other cities showed up for the mass and followed us to the cemetery. I didn't know most of them, but it was clear their affiliation with my father and our family's business. I watched as they lowered the two caskets into the ground and stayed until both were covered in dirt. I made the symbol of the cross over my body and bowed my head as I said my final goodbye.

The cemetery manager came up to me when it was all done. "The grass'll take a while to grow."

"When will my brother's stone be ready?"

"Week or two."

"And when will my parents' include my father's death date?"

"Week or two."

"Make it a week," I demanded. "Money is no object on this matter."

"Yes, ma'am."

Cristiano waited for me at the gate of the cemetery, and we walked back to our family home. The church was only a block from the cemetery and our home was three blocks past the church. He walked beside me, two of his men ten paces behind us.

"We meet with their lawyer tomorrow?"

"Yes, he will read the will and start all the proceedings. How long will you stay in Chicago?"

"I will stay with Nonno," I told him, trying to appease him. I love Auntie Ellen and Uncle David with them is my home, but without my mother or father or Angelo, someone needs to care for Nonno. "He needs someone to take care of him in the final days."

"And after Nonno dies?"

I shrugged, looking back at the two men following us. "I'm not sure."

The house was flooded with people when we got there. The kitchen is full of food, and good Italian wine being passed around as people dressed in black drank and laughed. Cristiano left me promptly when we got back to the house, going to see his friends within our organization. Today is about politics for him, he has to get my father's advisors behind him to take over. Yet, if the enforcers don't like him, I can't image the advisors do either.

The wives came up to me, comforting me for my losses. Nonno sat in the dining room, surrounded by older gentlemen that remember a time when he ran this city and it was drugs, not booze, we peddled.

"Miss Sanna?" I turned from the food surrounding the kitchen to the tall women behind me. She was soft in all her features, tall with the palest hair I'd ever seen.

"Yes?"

"I hate to intrude..."

"No, no please, what is your name?"

"I'm Irene Di Pietro, my father worked for yours very closely for years."

"It is lovely to meet you, Irene. Is your father here?"

"Yes, he's with your nonno," she pointed him out, sitting next to the old man in the dining room. He was laughing, speaking to Nonno in fluent Italian. "He wants to speak to you."

"Alright," I set down my drink and Irene stopped me.

"Not now," Irene stepped between me and her father. She handed me a slip of paper. "Tomorrow let's have breakfast at our house. The address is on the card. Mary will be here to take care of your nonno."

The maid I knew was here during the week to clean and care for him. I met her on Wednesday when I arrived, and we've spoken about his care in the past few days. She has the weekends free, but she came yesterday to help me prepare the house for the enormous number of guests we've had today.

"My father has coffee imported from *Italia*, it is divine," she said next as my cousin entered the kitchen.

"Addy, there are some people I'd like you to meet," Crisitano drug me away, but Irene gave me a reassuring smile.

I stood outside the Di Pietro house the next morning; it was only a few blocks away and I left as soon as Mary arrived. It stood tall, a striking red brick that made it the centerpiece of the block. I knocked on the door and Irene opened it. "Welcome, Miss Sanna."

"Please call me Addy," I offered her. She led me through her home to the dining room where his parents sat. Pictures on the wall showed more siblings than just Irene, but no one else was present at the table. Mrs. Di Pietro poured me a cup of coffee and offered me breakfast. Serving her husband, myself, and Irene before she made her own plate.

"Miss Sanna, let me begin by telling you how sorry I am for your loss. I blame myself for not being with your father that day," Mr. Di Pietro began as he sipped his coffee. "I looked forward to the day your brother ran our group, he would have done a good job. Your father raised him right."

"Thank you," I replied awkwardly. Everyone gave me condolences, but these were two men I did not know. I was as much a stranger to my brother and father as I am to the man in front of me.

"As you may know, with your father having no other sons, it is assumed your cousin Cristiano Sanna will take over as the head of your family."

"I do know this."

"I do not like your cousin," Mr. Di Pietro said bluntly. My gaze shot at him, and we shared a long stare. "I do not want him as my boss."

"What do you mean?"

"If he begins ordering me around, I will likely kill him and leave this city," he threatened casually. Threats are common in this world though, so in place with how it all works. Yet I wasn't raised in this world, and my heart races with the threat. Would he kill me with such ease as he threatens my cousin?

"Cristiano has no brothers; I have no other male cousins on my father's side. Do you propose yourself to take over the Sanna's rule over Chicago?"

"I propose you, Miss Sanna."

"Me?" I glace at Irene wearily. "As the head of a mafia family?"

"You, with my support and guidance."

"So, really you, with my name," I replied, lifting my head to meet his gaze. He wants to use me as a figurehead. "You only want my name on your deeds."

"No, Miss Sanna, I want you to run it. You will be our boss in every way, but you'll need help. Your father needed help too, and so did your grandfather. You don't fully understand this world because you were raised down in, what was it?"

"Monticello."

"You didn't learn how to run the mafia in Monticello, but you could learn. I can teach you," he offered with a slight smile. He really hates Cristiano if he's proposing a woman take over the Italian mafia's holdings in Chicago.

"How would it work?"

"Today, the will your parents made will be read. It lists you as the primary and sole beneficiary since Angelo is gone. Cristiano is only mentioned in that he gets nothing," he began, taking a bite of his breakfast. "Cristiano will want you to sign him over the rights to the lounges, warehouses, and commercial vehicles your parents owned for his use in our operation."

"And I refuse him."

"Precisely, you maintain ownership of the Sanna fortunes then you maintain ownership of the mafia. You will rule this city."

"What's the catch?" I asked him suspiciously. I looked over his wife, his daughter; he didn't want Cristiano to know I came here. He doesn't trust my cousin. Felix and Bruno obviously didn't want him as a boss. Why? Did they think

I would be easier to control, easier to manipulate. Maybe Mr. Di Pietro has some of the men in his pocket, let me be afraid about Cristiano so I would maintain my inheritance.

I feared Cristiano would cash in his favor for my hand, marrying me to the highest bidder. Di Pietro may do the same, women don't fully inherit, my husband would gain control of all my property once I wed. It is possible an invisible war is being fought amongst the Sanna mafia higher ups, a war for control over my marriage. Mr. Di Pietro is probably only the first in a line of my father's advisers wanting control over that decision. Cristiano introduced me to many yesterday, and some of them looked at me like a lamb brought to slaughter. A few of them want me for themselves.

"No catch, I just do not like Crisitano."

"There is always a catch, always a deal to be made. That is how this works," I reminded him. I'm not stupid. I may not have been raised in this life, but I know it.

"Irene becomes your assistant, a job."

"A job?" I turned to Irene. Her bright blue eyes and pearl smile reflect back at me.

"Yes, keep her close and keep me close. Let us help you though this time, and if there is ever a time you don't want our company, we will leave."

I glared at him with caution. All these men will want to take advantage of me, I must remind myself of that. I know none of them, I cannot trust any of them. That includes Mr. Di Pietro and

Cristiano.

"Cristiano will try to kill me if I don't sign over those properties."

"Your father's men will be loyal to you, just as they were your brother. No one blames you for being raised downstate, in fact, many admire your parents for their decision to separate you from this life."

"If I have the property and the men, then why does Cristiano think he's getting it all?"

"Because your cousin is selfish and stupid. It is why none of us want him as a boss."

CHAPTER 3

Adelaide Sanna

"There has to be a mistake," Cristiano fumed as we sat with the lawyer. He read the will, saying it was only my late brother and myself that my parents left anything it. As Mr. Di Pietro told me, it's all mine. Cristiano has been left nothing.

"No mistake, the will of Mr. Luciano Sanna lists Angelo Sanna as the primary beneficiary and Adelaide Sanna as the secondary. With the proof of Angelo's death certificate, it all passes to Miss Sanna. As far as we can tell, there is no record that Angelo had a will, and since he has no wife or children, all that would have been his became Miss Sanna's," the lawyer explained it all once more for Cristiano. I hide my smirk, watching him throw a fit over it all. Proof that what Mr. Di Pietro told me is true, he is selfish.

My cousin asked if there is any way to overrule the will. After all, I am a woman. Why should I be entitled to an inheritance? I wanted to scoff at the behavior, but instead I just sit and listen. Silent and polite, just like Auntie Ellen taught me. The lawyer explains that most of it will be held in a trust, not mine to sell and his to maintain, but mine to profit from. When I marry, the trust will be dissolved, and everything will belong to my husband. Mr. Di Pietro told me yesterday he'd say that, but the lawyer worked only for the mafia. He's under my thumb now, just like everything else in Chicago.

We left the lawyer, me having made another appointment to go over my estate and sign paperwork. Cristiano was bubbling with anger, his face turning redder and redder as we drove back to the family's house.

He dropped me there before leaving, letting me celebrate my small victory. It could all be mine, just like Mr. Di Pietro told me. This entire branch of the Italian Mafia could be under my control in a matter of days. The empire my nonno built in Chicago passes to me, not my cousin. Irene waited for me in the house, holding ledger books and property details.

"It was as your father said," I told her, and we entered the house. "The fortune, the properties, the cars, and boats. It all remains with me. Cristiano has nothing."

It shouldn't satisfy me to know he has nothing. A week ago, I hadn't even wanted it. I didn't even know it was possible for me to have it. I always knew Angelo would inherit the business.

I thought eventually that I'd be summoned back to Chicago to marry for the good of the family. Now I'd marry for my own good. My choice. No doubt Mr. Di Pietro would offer to help me, he would want to influence the outcome of my nuptials. After all, it is now my choice on who will rule Chicago after my father. My husband will own this part of the Italian Mafia. My choice, not Cristiano's or Angelo's. I make the next Sanna King.

"I've taken the liberty of making a list of your establishments you'll want to visit. You'll need to make yourself known to the staff as the new owner. I've completed a schedule for you in order of the success and tenure of the businesses," she began as we sat in the study my father kept on the first floor. *His* office, now *my* office. Right off the parlor and painted a rich blue, the study featured dark wood furniture and shelving.

His family ring still sat on his desk, waiting to be waved around and used to indent someone's jaw. I took it in my hands. Examining the Sanna crest from the old country. His hands were big. This ring used to sit on his middle finger, but I slip it onto my thumb. "In total, your family owns six lounges within Chicago, two shipment yards with respective docks and warehouses, six boats, and three motorcars."

"That sounds like a lot," I sighed, relaxing into father's black leather chair and still staring at the ring.

"Your father and brother have it divided

into smaller families the held shares within the individual companies. You'll want to meet with them, make a show of power."

"What does your father run?"

"Security operations. He maintains the enforcers and hires the goons that work club security and dock management. He also is your fixer, for when people become problems."

I nodded along with her, "Interesting. Go on."

"Ciro Renzi manages the warehouses, he's... tricky."

"Tricky how?"

"Well, my father did some reconnaissance for you before your arrival, focusing on who would follow a female boss. Renzi is a real traditional man, and you'll have to make a show of it for him. He'll need convincing."

"How do I do that?" Kill someone on my first day?

"This is a man's game, Miss Sanna. To play a man's game you have to act like a man. No emotion, no weakness. Renzi can come around, and if he doesn't..."

"He becomes an example," I finished for her. This will be harder than I thought. It isn't just freedom I'm gaining in this arrangement, but responsibility. If I let this family become weak, then it doesn't just mean a loss of that freedom again, but for any mafia daughter after me.

That night, after listening to Irene's analysis of how my family's part of the mafia runs, we both dressed in our evening wear and went to my biggest money maker: *Claudia*. A club in the central downtown location. Tonight, an up-and-coming pianist would be playing to entertain crowds while drugs and booze are sold under the table. It was a true longue, no wild dancing or jazz. Just a nice place to sit, listen to music, play cards, and drink. Luca, one of the younger guards, drove us there in my mother's favorite: the Crane-Simplex Model 5.

We got there an hour before opening, so I could meet my staff. The manager was one Marvin Ackmann, a German originally from St. Louis. He was a fat man, with short little legs, but from what Irene told me a hell-of-a longue manager. We walked in, Luca following close behind us and make our way to the bar where Marvin sat with the longue ledger.

"Luca? What is this? Who is this?"

They don't know me. None of them will. I wasn't raised in Chicago like my brother. No, my parents shipped me downstate to be raised on a farm by my aunt and uncle with their children. They loved me like their own, and we had been a happy little family. I planned to live my whole life downstate. My whole life as a farm girl, and eventually a farm wife. Despite knowing I'd likely be sold off as a *principessa mafiosa da premio.*

That part of my life had to die though. I couldn't be sweet or naïve anymore. If I wanted to do this, then proving myself to my organization was first on the list. I needed to play the man's game, but maybe with a feminine flare. Honey will catch me more flies than vinegar, and I don't need to act ruthless until I'm given a reason.

"Mr. Ackmann," I greeted him with a smile. "It is a pleasure."

He smiled back, a sly smile that had my spine shivering. I didn't like the way he watched me approach him, or how he didn't stand to greet me. If I were my father, he'd have stood. "And who might you be, miss?"

"Miss Sanna, Adelaide Sanna in fact and if we want to be precise, I am the new owner of this establishment and your boss," I glared at him, giving a little vinegar. "And you will stand to greet me."

Marvin scrambled to his feet then, "Miss Sanna, a pleasure to meet you. We- we weren't expecting our new owner for a few weeks. I- I- may I offer you a drink?"

I sat next to where he had been sitting, "Not right now, maybe when the pianist arrives and plays, I will indulge in one. For now, let us speak business. Under normal days you answer to a Cristiano Sanna, correct?"

"Yes, ma'am. Him or your brother, God rest

his soul. I- I am sorry for your loss, miss."

"Thank you. You will no longer answer to my cousin. Until further notice when there is an issue it will be brought directly to me. I can be reached through Miss Di Pietro," I explained sharply. Irene said the first thing I need to do is cutting Cristiano out of operations so he cannot vie for support amongst my men. Mr. Di Pietro made sure all my guards were loyal to me, more specifically to him, while the transition was occurring. Luca was close with Angelo and was his guard and friend. Stood with him the day my brother died and tried to protect him during the police shootout.

"Directly to you?"

"Yes, I'll also be wanted the ledgers from the last six months, I want to check on how *Claudia* is being run," I continued. I go over my new policies, such as an increase in his security for the next month as things get settled and the fact that ledgers will be sent to me monthly for review. It isn't that I don't trust him, Irene said he does his jobs well, but putting limits on them will make them know I'm not weak or malleable. It will make them squirm a little and encourage them to earn my favor. It will show that I demand the same respect given to my father and brother when they walked into this longue.

Two hours later, I found myself relaxing in an Italian leather chair with Irene and a few regulars joining me as we drank and conversed.

Irene introduced me to Mr. Richmond, who I knew as the Deputy Mayor of Chicago. He and his wife joined our table. They'd be coming to *Claudia* for years to listen to the music and when they'd heard this pianist would be here, they knew they had to attend. Though, judging by the glass in Mr. Richmond's hand, it wasn't just the music that drew their attendance.

Mr. Di Pietro and his wife joined us later into the night, after the Deputy Mayor left. They sat with us, discussing the particularly warm May weather and the Sonata in C Major that the pianist was playing. Business wasn't discussed, as Irene warned me before they arrived, no shoptalk in the open. We would retire to the upstairs offices if Mr. Di Pietro needed to speak with me about work.

When Cristiano walked in, I knew my evening of relaxing was coming to an end. He strode up to me, two men following directly behind him. His brows furrowed, and his eyes looked dangerous in the candle-lit room. For the first time in my life, I feared my cousin.

I stood to greet him on instinct, "Cousin."

"Addy," he growled. His voice was laced with disrespect and hatred. I sat now where he wanted to sit his whole life. "We need to talk?"

"Can it wait?"

"It cannot." With that, he turned and left the main longue room for the back staircase that led up. I tried to steady my hands and heart, both trembling. My auntie raised me to do as I was told, and to be a good wife I'd have to learn to bend to the will of men. Now, I'd have to forge my own path, Cristiano would try to gain control over me, and I couldn't let him have it.

I turned to Mr. Di Pietro, hoping he'd accompany me upstairs to inform my cousin he would not gain control of the mafia's holdings in Chicago. The older gentlemen nodded, turning to summon Luca and Felix who stood waiting by the wall. Together, me and the three men went up to the office spaces on the second floor.

"Cristiano, what is this about?" I asked, successfully keeping my voice even as I sat on the plush couch in the dark room. Piano music still wafted in the air, as Cristiano stood by the far wall, tense. Mr. Di Pietro came inside, sitting beside me while Luca stood in the doorway and Felix in the hall by the stairs.

"You too, Di Pietro?"

"I have no idea of what you're talking about, Sanna."

"I'm talking about this conspiracy to take what is rightfully mine!" Crisitano bellowed, making me flinch. "Angelo is dead, you answer to me!"

"I answer to Luciano's heir, that is not you."

He almost started yelling again, but I stood to stop him. I can't let Mr. Di Pietro speak for me. I have to establish control. I have to play the men's game the way my father and brother did. "It was their wish to give it all to me."

"You're a woman," he growled. "Not even raised in Chicago, you don't know the first thing about being a mafia boss."

"That may be true," I glanced over my shoulder to Mr. Di Pietro. "But I will learn. I will do right by my father's legacy, my grandfather's legacy."

"He's using you," Cristiano voiced a thought I already had. He may be using me, but he has also been up front with me and honest. His intentions are clear whereas Cristiano's are a blur. I can either let Cristiano use me, or I can let Di Pietro use me. Only one is promising something resembling a choice. "You need to sign the longues, the docks, all of it over to me. Let me have what is mine."

"No."

"No?" My hand starts to tremble, so I fold them across my chest. No fear, no weaknesses. "You can't tell me 'no,' Adelaide."

"I just did, Cristiano," I spat back. "Get behind me or get out of my city."

"You will start a war by doing this. Do you want a war?"

"I want your respect," I fired off. My heart raced, this time not with fear but with anger. I deserve his respect. I deserve this choice.

"You cannot do this," he took a step towards me, grabbing both my shoulder and gripping hard. I want to wince, but I know I cannot. These men, my father's men, they don't want him as their leader. He is not worthy; I can be worthy. "He will marry you off to the highest bidder and use your marriage to forever control Chicago."

"As if that wasn't your plan."

His fingers dig into my arms, biting into my skin with his nails. Just as I think he will truly hurt me, he backs off, "Bendoni won't stand for this." He doesn't say it to me, he says it to Mr. Di Pietro.

All the man does is smile, holding up his hand and make a 'come here' gesture with two fingers to the men behind Cristiano. The follow his order, moving from behind my cousin to my side.

Mr. Di Pietro rose, "All the power you think you have was given to you by me and your uncle. I'm taking it back now, on behalf of Luciano. I know where my loyalties lie, and so do these men. You have no one backing you, Sanna. Now, I believe boss here gave you a choice, pledge your loyalty to her or get out of her God damn city."

Cristiano's eyes burn, his hands clenched tight at his side. He won't follow me; he doesn't see what Mr. Di Pietro sees in me. While I don't know what my father's advisor sees either, I can feel it now. I can feel the power he sees in me, the possibilities I possess. I feel it as the anger courses through me, and I contemplate what I'll have to do if Cristiano refuses. I can be strong enough to lead this city, because I'm already contemplating killing for this position.

Cristiano leaves. He stomped out of the room, leaving me with the two men that escorted him inside. I turned then to both men that had stood by my side while I faced him, those that betrayed him. "You two are staying."

"There is no choice, boss. You're Sanna's heir, you're our new boss."

"Good, tell the others. I want the whole of Chicago to know who I am by morning."

"Yes, boss," the other one says, both leave.

I then addressed Mr. Di Pietro, "Was he right, about a war?"

"No one will touch you while I'm live. I won't make the mistake I made with your father and brother."

CHAPTER 4

Noè Bendoni

Elio and I waited for the visitors that came around this time of year. May was a popular time for the heads of the families around the country to visit with us, catch us up on the ongoings across the country. In July, padre would go over to Italia and give a full report on the mafia's holdings in the United States. Before he left, many of the family heads or their eldest sons would meet with us here in New York to update us on their operations.

Before us sat the head of our Detroit branch, Gabriele Adesso. He was a middle-aged man, married to one of my cousins, making him blood. We drank and shared stories of the past year. His third son was born and named after my padre, like a true *leccaculo*. Just like the rest of the family heads. Half of them had daughters or nieces who'd they'd talk about, trying to sell them to us. Gabriele didn't have any daughters, and his sisters were both married already, meaning we could simply relax and converse with this man. Elio and I were both unmarried, although Elio had been promised to the mafia princess in *Italia* since he was six. Yet I'm available, unattached, and if my padre has anything to say on it, I'd be matched soon with a mafia-blooded female. Meaning these meetings were just as much about seeing all the eligible mafia ladies as much as knowing the state of our business.

Thankfully with Gabriele I could be at ease.

Elio began to pour us another round when the door was thrown open. I drew my gun in an instant, training it on the man who burst in. Two of my guys follow, grabbing his arms. The intruder fought them, "Let me go. *Ne me touche pas.*" He shrugged off their hands, when he starts to scream at them in Italian. "I have a right to be here."

"Who are you?" Elio demanded; his own gun pulled on the man.

"Cristiano Sanna, of the Chicago Sanna family."

I lowered my gun, "Mr. Sanna. I heard your uncle and cousin died. A shooting by police." I nodded to Elio, confirming that this *testa di cazzo*, was in fact one of ours.

"I apologize for this intrusion," Elio said to Gabriele. "Please leave us."

Gabriele glared at Sanna, not like the blatant disrespect he's displayed. I returned to my seat, downing the liquor Elio had poured me. "Sit, Sanna."

He did as I said, Elio sitting beside me, glaring, "Obviously there is some issue you believe is urgent."

"Yes, there is an issue I'm having with the leadership of the Chicago enterprise. You need to hold that city and I have concerns about who Luciano left to carry on his name," Sanna began, his leg twitching and his fist clenched tight.

"It isn't you?" I poured myself another drink, sipping this one instead of downing it. As far as I knew, Luciano Sanna only had one son, and of course, his daughter. I knew little of his daughter, but he spoke of her kindness last year when he visited. Like many mafia fathers, he longed to make her a good match, and I was the catch of the Italian mafia since my brother is unavailable.

"No. My uncle was obviously a foolish man, he named his daughter, Adelaide Sanna, as his heir and the *puttana* think she's entitled to what is mine."

"What makes you think it's your title?" I grumbled, swirling the amber gold in my glass.

"I am Sanna's nephew, his only son is dead!"

"Don't yell at me, boy." He is probably older than me, judging by the few wrinkles that litter his forehead. "Tell me straight."

"She isn't worthy. She has no right to be in that position. This is due to one of Luciano's men, he doesn't like me because I courted his daughter, so now he's trying to put me in my place by cheating me out of my right."

"You must be a small man to let a little girl take your 'right,'" Elio snarked, chucking lightly at the man in front of us. He didn't like Elio's reaction to the story he's told. If this man, a grown man who worked for the Italian mafia most of his life, lost his assumed inheritance to a girl, then he must be weak.

From what I remember of Adelaide Sanna, she was raised in central Illinois, away from her family's business. He always said he received letters about her wellbeing; she is smart according to Luciano. Nineteen years old and a beauty, like Mrs. Sanna had been in her youth. We had no doubt that he'd come here this year ready to marry her off, we had expected it since Mrs. Sanna passed in January. Now her cousin sat here, with entirely unexpected news of Miss Sanna's doings. She's running the Sanna Mafia family. It makes want me laugh.

"Luciano Sanna left it all to her?" I asked next.

"Apparently, but this has his right-hand man's work all over it. I don't believe my uncle would do this."

"If you can't get one man to follow you, obviously you don't deserve the position," I smirked as I waited for his reaction.

"I want to speak to your father. This issue should be brought to him."

"No offense, Sanna," Elio stood, stalking over to Sanna as he spoke. My older brother grabbed his arm, pulling him out of the chair. A move reminiscent of my father. "This issue doesn't even belong to us. You lost your position to a girl, and that girl has her entire enterprise's backing. You're not strong enough to lead the Sanna family. I recommend you go home and beg that little girl to not kill you for coming here like this. Any other mafia boss would see it as a betrayal."

Elio threw him out, ordering the guards to put him back on a train to Chicago. The door slams shut. "What kind of courting do you think he did to get Di Pietro that pissed at him."

"The kind of courting that would lead to us overlooking his death were it to occur," Elio replied, causing me to nod. "I don't like men that disrespect ladies. Not Di Pietro's daughter nor Sanna's."

"We sent our condolences to the miss, didn't we?"

"Padre sent flowers and a case of bourbon."

"I got a letter from Luciano Sanna in February," I told him. I kept it from him and padre, not wanting to bring it up prematurely. "He was trying to have me call on Chicago this summer and court her while padre is in *Italia*. Merge our families and strengthen our bonds." My grandfather knew hers back in the home country. Bendoni and Sanna are two names known among the elites back home. Strong names and strong families.

"You want Chicago?"

"No," I denied, knowing exactly his train of through. Anyone she married became the holder of her inheritance now. I'm sure when Luciano proposed the match, he didn't foresee a future where the young miss was left a sole inheritor of the business. If I go after Adelaide Sanna, I've assured myself to rule her family's mafia kingdom.

"You considered it?"

"Her mama had just died, I knew Sanna just wanted to assure her a good future. I told myself if he came here with her this May, I'd take her out, court her, and see where it went from there." Padre would approve of this match, even now. I was his spare in case anything happened to Elio, but if he could place one son as the King in New York and another on the Chicago throne, it would expand our family's power.

My drink emptied into the back of my throat. It burned as it went down, but it warmed my stomach and made the thought of the girl go away. "Let's be done for the day."

CHAPTER 5

Adelaide Sanna

"C risitano went to New York," Irene told me as soon as she walked into my home. I gave her a key and open access; over the past two weeks she's seemed to be stuck to my side and the house can get lonely with only me and Nonno.

She's five years older than me yet has already become a close friend. I don't know if she's been nice to me because of her father's orders, but at this point I don't care. I'm alone in Chicago, with no real family or familiarity. So having her kindness has been nice. Plus, she seemed genuinely interested in helping me run this city and hasn't led me astray yet.

"Straight to the boss," I shook my head. He'd mention Bendoni in our argument at *Claudia*, and afterward Di Pietro told me about the American head of the Italian mafia. Bettino Bendoni ruled the Italian mafia's branches here in the states and reported back to the true King of it all back in

Italia.

"Not exactly, Felix's cousin's brother-in-law works for Elio Bendoni, he sent word that Cristiano couldn't get to the big man, had to deal with the boys." The boys, Bendoni's two sons, that have helped him rule New York and the states since they were fourteen. "They sent him packing. No word from Cristiano since. He's gone silent."

"Keep Felix working on it, I want to know where he is, when he leaves, and where he's going," I ordered her. Irene nodded and turned to leave, before I stopped her. "No one ever told me why they don't like him. I assume he's *un proco Giuda,* but no one ever told me."

"I will tell you anything," Irene assured me. She's said many times that she's will always be on my side. With her help, the men of this city are bending to my will. I'm starting to believe she won't forsake me.

"Sit." I grab a bottle of whiskey and pour two glasses. Irene sets down her purse on the coffee table and takes her drink. "Tell me."

"Cristiano and I were together for a time, when we were both younger," she explained to me slowly. "We were going out once, to one of the clubs your father owned. On our way there we got intercepted by some guy from the Irish side of the city. It seemed like they knew each other. Afterwards I asked him about it, and he told me to learn my place: to look pretty and shut up. I brought it up to my father, and he confronted

Cristiano. He was... he..."

"He has a temper," I inferred.

"Yes, and he was *incazzado...* he hit me," Irene drowned her drink down then. "Left a fat bruise. My father would have killed him if yours hadn't stopped him. Mr. Sanna said it wasn't the time or place. That Cristiano was a Sanna, and he couldn't stand by and let a Sanna die. My father didn't speak to him for almost a month, so angry that he'd let the man that hurt me go unpunished. He's been punished now."

"What kind of man was my father?"

"The man that protected his family, that's why he didn't let mine kill Cristiano." I shook my head, ready to say something. Say that he shouldn't have protected Cristiano after he hit her. That her father should have killed him. It is all on the tip of my tongue, but I don't say it because she spoke again, "My father said the mafia was our family, that Mr. Sanna taught him that. He protected his family by making you the heir. He kept us all from Cristiano's reign. He told me before you came here, we had to do everything we could to help you, that Mr. Sanna set it up, but we had to see it through."

"You think my father wanted him alive to know he would lose everything?"

"What I know is that when your Uncle Ivan made Mr. Sanna promise to protect his son, and your nonno made it Sanna law that no internal murders would occur without the boss's approval."

"He knew Cristiano would be punished, just not with his death."

"Yes. He intended it to be whenever Angelo took over. Angelo planned to keep Cristiano close, but not powerful. Keep him in check by making him learn his place below him, but not strong enough to garner support to take over."

"Cristiano won't stay gone. He'll come back," I leaned back into the sofa. "He won't stop trying to claim what he sees as his, and in his eyes, Chicago belongs to him."

CHAPTER 6

Adelaide Sanna

1924

"Police, everyone stops what you're doing!" I look up from my ledger for our newest club to open: Petit Coeur. I step back from the halfway built bar. Four officers enter the club, I recognize one as my own, it is his partner that approaches me.

"Good morning," I say with a bright smile, ready to offer the officers some honey. "What can I do for Chicago's finest today?"

"Ma'am we need to speak of the owner of this building," the officer says as he stops in front of me.

"He's not here, I'm the manager of this establishment. My grandfather owns this building, but I'm the manager of his estates. All my paperwork is there on the bar."

He goes to grab the papers, sifting through them all. Two of the officers he's brought with him start to meander around the main room of the unopened club. My eyes dart to the cop on my payroll and I glare. He should have warned me about this. "We have it on good authority that bootlegging' has occurred in this building, we want to search the premise."

"Bootlegging? Officer, I assure you that this is a dry building."

"Even so, can we have a look around?"

"Anywhere you'd like," I offer, gesturing to the building. "I abhor alcohol personally, so if you find any, I will personally help in any way I can to figure out where it came from. We are set to open in three weeks as a dancing club. I would hate for something like alcohol to set back our opening."

The officer nods to the two others and they start to search the club, plus the backroom. There is an upstairs too, which they will no doubt want to look at. Either way, they won't find a drop today... tomorrow would have been worse. My shipments for this club come in tonight.

"Any of the employees here known for bootleggin?"

"If they were they won't be employees," I lie to him. I've become very good at lying. It was one of the first thing Di Pietro made me learn. "I'm a devote Catholic and feel that any alcohol, outside the Lord's supper, is what has run this great nation into the dirt. All these young kids are our getting tipsy and committing crime. That's why my grandfather owns clubs like these, a safe, *dry*, establishment where the good folks of Chicago can have fun without that kind of influence."

I've gotten good at this over the years. Cops see me and believe just about anything I say to them. I'm an innocent woman; any alcohol they find couldn't be mine. It must be one of those construction workers, or a waitress who's getting funny on the job. A few of my employees have fallen over the years to prohibition laws, but we always get them a good lawyer to help out.

"How many of these establishments does your grandfather own?"

"This is number eight. Oh, officer you have to come visit our piano longue *Claudia*," I gush, placing my hand on his arm. Now is the time to do some name dropping, "The Deputy Mayor comes in every Friday to play a round of cards with me."

"Excuse me, miss, can we go upstairs?" one of the other officers comes in to ask. I give him a happy nod, and he leaves with the officer who is leading the witch hunt. I drop my smile and glare at Officer Scott who has been in my pocket for two years.

"What is this?" I ask lowly as I move to stand near him.

"My partner got a tip that a shipment of booze was coming in for the new club. I was able to change the date on our report that the shipment came in last night instead of tonight. That way when we came in for the search, I knew nothing would be here," he explains quickly. "I'm sorry about short notice."

"No notice, Scott. You gave no notice. You're lucky I was here today."

"Yes, ma'am."

"Who is the rat?"

"I don't know a lot; he works at your docks, and my partner calls him Big Foot."

Big Foot? I wouldn't know him, but I'd find him and make sure the rat never squeaked again. "I want this new partner of yours dead."

"He's from the boonies, doesn't know how it works up here yet. Let me have some time with him, I can make him see your way." He looks down at me and meets my eyes. He looks sympathetic, Scott always looks sympathetic. It's what makes him so easily bought.

"You have a month. No more searches."

"I will see to it personally, ma'am."

"Good boy," I give him a wide smile. "Bring Lucy to the opening in a few weeks. You two will love it."

"Will do," he says as the other three finish their search.

"We didn't find anything," the partner says to Office Scott. "We are sorry to intrude, have a good day, miss."

"And you too officer." They leave, and I wave for one of the guys to lock the front door. No more intrusions for today. We open in three weeks; I need no delays.

Irene watches me, waiting for my next

move, "Scott said the rat is called Big Foot. I want him found and held. He's a traitor."

"I'll have Bruno look into it." Irene has spent the past three years by my side, and she's proved her worth to me every day.

"Don't let Bruno kill him. I want to be there to condemn this *verme*."

"Of course."

"And the docks tonight, have Luca do a thorough sweep before the shipment arrives. I want no personal there that we don't trust. No new guys."

"Are you still planning on going personally?"

"Yes, this won't shake me."

"It hasn't shaken you," she reminds me. I give her a glance, a small smile, then it is dropped. She's my rock. Irene helped me keep up appearances, always reminding me who I need to be around the men. Reminding me I'm doing this for my legacy and my family, and not one of them will follow me if I get hysterical.

"Tell Romano that if Scott's partner isn't on our payroll by opening, he is to disappear." I don't want Scott to know, I gave him a month but maybe he won't blame me if it happens before that. Violence ran the streets of Chicago, and I had men that specializes in making hits look like Irish kills. Scott would never know I ordered the hit; he'd blame the Irish which would push him more under my control. "Go home for now, Irene. I'm going to check on Nonno."

"You have a meeting with--"

"I know," I give her one last smile.

I leave the half-renovated club, having Luca drive me back to my home on Gold Coast. Over three years I've continued to build what Nonno started back in 1859 when Chicago was still an up-and-coming city. What my father builds in the early 1900's and now what I would build for my legacy. In three years, I've opened a new club on the upper east side of Chicago and started renovations on the building that would count as the eighth club owned by the Sanna family. Most of it was done in Nonno's name, since I as a woman couldn't do most of the legal work necessary without stamping his name on it.

Nonno has aged in these three years, losing more mobility in his arms and his speech is slurred. His memory has gone bad, and I've hired Mary's fifteen-year-old daughter to live-in with us full time. Mary still comes to clean, since Beth's primary job is Nonno's care.

I find them on the front porch, Beth reading Bible verses to him in Italian. It helps him, we think. It is too hard to take him to mass on Sundays, so Beth reads him scripture and Father David comes every Wednesday to give him absolution. His head was tilted up to the sun when I walk through the front gate, half the time he thinks I'm his sister or Nonna. Sometimes he thinks he's back in Italia and doesn't understand why everyone is speaking English.

"*Buongiorno, Nonno,*" I greet him with a kiss to his cheek. His gaze still trained at the sky; he doesn't greet me back. "Has he spoken at all today?"

"He asked me to read him Psalms," Beth says to me, closing Nonno's Bible but leaving her finger in the place she was reading from. "And this morning he asked for your nonna at breakfast."

I kneel beside him, putting myself at his eye level, "*Nonno, mi conosci?*"

"*Che? Ciao cara, buongiorno,*" he grabs my hand, patting it twice.

"Has he eaten?" I ask next.

"Oatmeal and a biscuit and jam," Beth says next. It was a routine for us. She knew all the questions and always had my answers. "Someone said the cops came to the new place today."

"They did, but there were no issues. When did he wake up?"

"About nine-thirty. Mr. Di Pietro is inside."

I nod, standing fully, "Thank you."

She reopened the Bible, continuing where she left off in Psalms as I went to the front door. As she said, Di Pietro waited by the fireplace for me. His back to me, his shoulders tense. Three years aged him, made his hair go grey and wrinkles form on his hands. He wasn't as scary looking as he was when I first met him, but anyone who known the Sanna family organization knows to fear him.

"Cristiano is back in Chicago; he's been here for three days."

"And I'm just learning this now because?"

"Because I just learned it this morning, right around the time I heard the police visited *Petit Coeur*. He will be an issue." It is easy to understand the words he hasn't said. He wants permission to do what my father prevented from happening years ago, he wants to kill Cristiano.

"He will, but he should see Nonno one last time," I reply, making my wishes known. Cristiano is *un cazzo*, but he is my cousin. He is no traitor, just entitled, and once he sees how well I've done without him, maybe he'll give in and join me. I wanted to do this together three years ago. The younger me had hoped he might follow me, but I was wrong. I'd been wrong many times in learning how to run the Chicago Italian mafia, but I always believed letting Cristiano live was not one of those times. "Find him for me."

"Who tipped off the police?"

"Scott said he was called Big Foot," I answer, sitting on the sofa in the middle of the room. "Irene is putting Bruno on it."

"Good," he turns to me then, sitting across from me on a chair. "What about the May trip to New York, will you accompany me this year?"

I shake my head, folding my hands in my lap. I knew that every year we needed to report to the American head of the mafia, and the visit is coming up in just two months. For the past three years, I've always made Di Pietro do it for me. Something in me, some instinct, said the minute a

Bendoni laid eyes on me I would lose it all. Those three men have the power to make or break me. They've never interfered in my inheritance, but I fear them seeing me might result in a different sentiment. Cristiano must have begged them to intervene, but just because they didn't then, doesn't mean they won't now.

"And the files I gave you?"

I glared at him then. Every month he gives me a list of suitable men within the various mafia groups to marry. Every month the list is topped with the same name. While there are many reoccurring names, they always come in varying order of appeal, but it is clear Di Pietro has his favorite.

Noè Bendoni.

The second son to the man who could disinherit me from Chicago, take my throne and pass it along to Cristiano. I'm given new information on him every month. He's remained unmarried, despite being on the top of every mafia padre's list of bachelors for their daughters, nieces, and granddaughters.

Noè took out seventeen Irish mobsters last month in a raid on a warehouse his father wanted in New York. He took control of all the holdings and are distributing them along the cost for resale. He was gracious enough to send Chicago a shipment of the firearms he stole. It felt personal. All the booze and drugs that were found got shipped to the east coast cities. Chicago was the only in-land to get a present like this from him.

It felt like a slap in the face.

Last November he hung a police office in the alley behind his precinct for arresting two of his men. It was impressive, to say the least. He reads as a ruthless and cunning Italian gentleman.

Yet, admitting I was looking for a husband would be like admitting I couldn't do this on my own. The minute I marry, this all becomes his. I no longer sit the throne of the Chicagoan Italian mafia, it is his. The rational side of me says that if I marry and have children, then Crisitano never gets what he wants, and that brings a smile to my face. However, the stubborn part of me, the part Di Pietro says is exactly like my brother, doesn't want to give it all up to some man.

"You will have to get married eventually, the options will become either you choose, Bendoni chooses, or Cristiano takes it all."

CHAPTER 7

Noè Bendoni

"The police have been all up our asses lately and now I hear that principessa in Chicago got raided too," Padre bellows as he paces back and forth in his office. He called Elio and me in here to discuss the May visits, but then he heard about the police visiting one of the new Sanna clubs in Chicago. Now, he's screaming. Cops have been closing in, and we've heard from multiple families that rats are multiplying.

"She's done well in Chicago over the past three years," Elio reminds him. Despite her being the only female to run a mafia family, she's done well. Padre made us keep a close watch on her, meaning I've kept in constant correspondence with her right-hand: Di Pietro. He disliked her mostly because she's never shown her face in New York, padre doesn't like that kind of disrespect.

"I don't like it. One wrong move by the *principessa* and we lose Chicago to the *consanguinei irlandesi*," he fumes, slamming his hand on the dark wood desk. He points at me, "You said she'd be married by now, that one of ours would be running Chicago instead of her. You were wrong."

That is what I said, six months after she took over came her first mistake. Padre called for her removal then, but I assured him no female would hold the position long. Eventually, she'd get married, and Chicago would be run by a man again. Yet, three years have passed, and she is still an eligible bachelorette that many mafia sons have set their eyes on. She's made it clear courting is the furthest thought in her mind, but the minute she shows interest, second and third sons from all over the country will flock to her city to call on her to win her throne.

"I cannot control a *prima donna* no more than you can, padre. Plus, she does good, three years and only one police intrusion. My source says she's got half the department in her pocket."

"She should be able to run that city without buying it!"

"We bribe the Mayor and Governor of New York," Elio reminds him, making me smirk. Silently, he and I have been rooting for the *principessa* to succeed. Not supporting her physically or verbally, but entirely spiritually. Wanting her to succeed knowing Cristiano Sanna is the alternative. Neither of us like Cristiano Sanna.

"You both must think I'm too old, but I have

run this family, this country for decades. I do not trust this girl."

"This girl is Luciano Sanna's daughter," I add, reminding him of the man that put Miss Sanna in her position. Luciano was a good, loyal man. Hardworking and willing to do anything for the good of the greater mafia. This sometimes meant sharing his profits with less lucrative cities to help other families get on their feet. He funded the expansion of the mafia into Dallas, and Orlando.

"We've never met her," Padre answers, falling into his chair. "She cannot show her face in New York, why should I trust her?"

"She's probably scared you'll remove her as head of the Sanna operations," Elio suggests. "As you say, she is a woman and the only one to run a city for the mafia."

"If she is scared then she shouldn't be in her position."

"*Che due coglioni, padre!* All the family heads fear us, you'd be pissed if she was arrogant enough to not be scared," I argue with him. His glare is deadly. I am his son but that doesn't mean I'm not subject to his anger. If he decides to punish me for my outburst, then no one could stop him.

"You will vouge for her then. Go to Chicago, I want a full report on her business practices and your best assessment on if she is fit to continue as she has. Leave my sight." Padres waves us off, Elio and I both leaving his office.

My brother leads me down to the street, his hand on my shoulder, "You shouldn't anger him like that, remember what it did to you last time."

"*Mi ricordo, fratello*," I say back to him, shuttering at the memory. "He is right, someone should check on this *principessa*. No matter what I said in there, it is not right she has not presented herself to us yet." We all know it. Her second, Di Pietro, comes every year in her stead. Even he thinks she's been childish by not appearing before my padre. If she was smarter, she would have come the first year and made a show of strength. Now, it is too late, and the impression is made.

"I know, but he's always unfair with her. He doesn't send us to check up on all the other family's when they are having issues with the cops."

We walk the street; thousands of other New Yorkers by our side. He walked with me to the apartment I kept in the city, wanting to be away from our childhood home where padre still lives. My assistant is there, he never comes with me to meetings with padre, and I never want him there. I tell him I want a train ticket on the next one to Chicago and he nods, leaving to get it done. I lived in a small one-bedroom apartment in Brooklyn, a simple home to keep me away from our family's home in Greenwich Village.

"What will you tell her?" he asks while sitting on my sofa.

"Exactly the truth, that I'm there to check in

on her and tell her she needs to get married."

"Will you marry her?"

"What?" I turn in shock to my brother's suggestion, staring him down.

"You were considering it three years ago. Do you still consider her a possibility?"

Yes, but I won't tell him that. Di Pietro and I have stayed in contact, and I know he's vying for her to marry me. We both know it will be her choice though, and I do not foresee her choosing me.

"Not as much as I did. She wouldn't marry me anyway; she'll marry someone she can use as a front to continue running her business as she sees fit. A weaker man who she can control."

"How do you know so much about her?" Elio asks next, watching me grab my bags from the hall closet.

I never told him or padre that Di Pietro kept me updated on all her doings. They didn't need to know how closely I watched her. Every move and every decision were reported to me. Not because I didn't trust her, I was simply curious. I wanted to know if she'd be able to take a person's life when needed, if she would order the hit or do it herself. I wanted to know how she'd deal with disrespect amongst those who saw fit to question her. I wanted to know if she'd continue to bootleg or try and take the business legit. Any expectations I had she met or exceeded.

Di Pietro reported only two months after

she took over how she'd taken the hand of a thief that stole from her docks. Then he told me about how she had three cops killed for getting too close to a warehouse that stored fine Italian wine. She had them all drugged and left them bleeding and high in front of an Irish pub. Discrediting them and killing them in one swoop. Adelaide Sanna is ruthless when it comes to business.

I liked it.

Then there are the stories I get from her maid, Mary. Stories on how she takes care of her Nonno, the infamous Lucilio Sanna who grew delicate in his old age. Mary told me how Miss Sanna cared for every need of the old man, even hiring her daughter so that he would never be alone in the house. How s3he learned more *Italiano* so that she could speak to him when he forgot English. A caring side of her that was shared with me, a part that I almost didn't want to know about. It seemed too invasive to know that she ate dinner with him every night and had a Catholic priest come to visit him every week when he couldn't make it to mass. It was too intimate to know those details of her life, but I knew them nonetheless, I reveled in the words. Every time I got one of their letters, I sat for hours reading every word they'd carefully written.

"I have my ways."

"You've been spying on her," Elio retorts with a snort. "You're no better than father when it comes to this."

He is right, I did spy on her, but for all the wrong reasons.

CHAPTER 8

Adelaide Sanna

Luca warned me before I walked into the warehouse about what I'd find inside. I am supposed to meet my dock manager about the shipment that came two days ago. I postponed distributing it in case Officer Scott and his partner made another trip my any of my clubs. Tonight, it needed to be distributed though, supplies at the other establishments are running low. It is supposed to be a simple night, in and out.

Instead, I find my dock manager on his knees in front of my cousin. "Cristiano," I greet the man I haven't seen in three years.

"Addy," he smirks, knowing the position he put us both in. Marcos, my dock manager, was a good man, with a wife and kids back home waiting for him to return after this shipment is processed.

Luca and Felix stand close to my side, ready to step in front of a bullet for me. I knew seven other men stood at the warehouse perimeter, on my word they'd come in here and kill him. This situation was delicate though, no one needed to die tonight, although Cristiano would pay for the embarrassment he's causing me.

"You know, this is where it happened, where your father and brother were shot. I'm surprised you still use this place," he looks around, but his hold in Marcos is firm and the barrel of the gun is pressed to his temple. My dock manager doesn't look scared though, he stares at me directly, knowing that danger like this comes with the job. "I thought your feminine sentiments would make you sell it or burn it down."

"I know everything about this building, about all of my buildings," I inform him, choosing to ignore his taunt. I step towards him and Marcos. "Let him go."

"No, I like this position we're in," he chuckles. "I like that look in your eyes, you don't know what to do next."

"If you don't put down that gun then I know exactly what will happen next. Don't be stupid, Cristiano," I shake my head, giving him a warning. Behind him, two of my dock guards enter through the back room, their guns up and aimed at Cristiano's back.

"Heard the cops got you on their radar," Crisitano shifts, he's scared. He knows these guys will kill him the minute I saw the word. "Cops never had Angelo in their scope."

"Rats are breeding." I take another step forward, putting myself closer and closer to him.

He can't kill me, if I die, he has no chance to take my family's business from me. It would be too easy to kill me, he wants to see me lose it the way he did.

"Uncle Luciano never had such disloyalty. Your boys must be unhappy with their boss." His grip readjusts, Marcos watches me, waiting for me to get him out of my cousin's grip so he can go home to his family.

I can't act weak though, "Crisitano, we both know if you wanted to kill him, he'd be dead. I am a very busy woman, so kill him so my guys can kill you or drop your gun and leave."

He laughs, it is shaky and unsettling, "We both know I'm not leaving this building. I won't get the luxury of bleeding out in my bed like Luciano and Angelo. I will get no mercy even after everything I've done for you."

"You did do a lot for me," I admit, knowing everything he did after every death in of my immediate family. He helped father and Angelo after my mother's death. He covered up how they both died in the cop's reports. "I can repay you now. I am not without mercy."

"Then you're a weak boss." Gunshots ring out from outside, Luca grabs me, pulling me away from Cristiano as he re-aims his gun for my person. Luca grunts as a bullet flies through the air. Felix draws as well, firing back. I don't see any of it as Luca rushes me out of the warehouse. My driver lies dead on the pavement, but Luca throws me in the car and drives me off.

His shoulder bleeds onto the seat of the Model T as he drives me from the scene. "I didn't think--" I begin but stop. He won't want to hear it, and he would never question my decisions either way. In my purse, I pull out my handkerchief and press it to his shoulder. He takes me to my home, stopping out front.

"Go home."

"Luca, you need a doctor."

"I do, I will take care of it. Go home and be safe, I'm sure the other bosses will be by shortly."

"Don't baby me, Luca, I am no child."

"No," he turns to me. "You're the boss and all of us remember the last time a shooting happened at that warehouse. Let us deal with this, you deal with whoever is waiting for you in that house."

"Go to a doctor, that is an order."

"Yes, ma'am."

I get out of the car. Usually, my father's Ford stays at the house, but he will get to a doctor, one of our doctors, quicker in that car. I watch him drive off from the stoop, his blood staining my pants and blouse. I never liked these pants anyways. Inside, my top men waited for me. Di Pietro, in charge of my enforcers; Titone, in charge of my docks and the shipments; and Renzi, in charge of inventory and distribution to the longues. They all stood in my parlor, waiting for me. Irene sat at the chair, her eyes scanning over me and widening at the blood.

"Word travels fast."

"We met your father and brother here under different circumstances," Titone answers first. They all speak freely around me, often giving advice if I want it or not. It is a freedom they've always been afforded in the walls of this home and one I've never revoked.

"The blood?" Di Pietro refers to the stains on my clothing.

"Luca deserves a raise."

"Noted."

"Irene, please prepare a change of clothing, one appropriate to go to *Claudia* tonight," I ask, and she moves to go to my room.

"You're going out tonight?" Di Pietro asks.

"If you've heard no doubt it has spread to every level of the organization and outside," I explain, stepping further into the parlor. "I need to make a show of myself tonight to make sure everyone knows I'm alive tomorrow."

"It is a good plan," Renzi says more to the other two than me. "The workers will want to know she's alive, especially after her father and brother died from a shootout in that warehouse."

Titone chuckles, "We should burn down that building."

"Crisitano will pay for his betrayal," Di Pietro promises me, and I agree. He wasn't a traitor before, just stupid. With his actions today, Crisitano signed his death warrant.

"I want him dead, he had his last chance today," I tell him, all of them need to know that he may have my name, but he is no longer family. My family stands in his room, my family was shot because of his actions. Crisitano is no cousin of mine, his blood will spill, and I won't even honor him with a burial. He can rot in Lake Michigan. "He will pay for him crimes against this family."

They all nod and I go upstairs to change. Irene laid me out a black dress, long gloves and golden jewelry. I dressed, leaving the bloody clothing on the floor, saying "Burn it," to Irene as I pass her in the hallway. I leave the room, going down to see all three men still waiting for me. "What else is there?"

"He had help," Di Pietro tells me.

"Obviously, find out who. I want a full report in the morning." Ten men stand outside, Felix in the forefront of them. I look over each of them, they gathered here for me. To lay eyes on me just as I assumed they'd want too. The steps down the stoop feel steeper than they have before. Felix rushes to grab my hand, his head is cut open, a small tricking of blood dripping down his face.

"Boss." He grabs my arm as I finish the last step.

"Your head is bleeding, see to it that is stops," I give him a small smile. "Is he dead?"

"Fled the scene."

"Thank you," I pat his arm. "Take the night for yourself."

"Where you go, I go. That's the deal, boss."

"Then we are going to *Claudia*."

CHAPTER 9

Noè Bendoni

The longue was full, no chair sat empty in the whole place. Couples danced to the piano and violin duo while others played cards, gambled, and drank. I arrived in Chicago only a few hours ago, and after promptly checking into a hotel, I found myself walking to Claudia, what the concierge told me was the best longue to be on a Friday night. It also happened to be the most successful of the Sanna holdings. Two giant men were outside the door when I came, and two more stood inside. A quick glance around the main room of the club had me counting ten in total, more than one would expect of a simple Friday evening at the longue.

Miss Sanna must be here. Still, her presence might account for the two goons on the inside and general security for the two outside the door. Something else was going on here. Maybe it was the cops that were closing in, she wanted to be prepared. Then again, such a presence would only draw attention.

I casually stride further into *Claudia*, deciding to look for the woman and ask her. I'd never seen her before, but I've met her parents and brother, she can't look much different. The VIP section of the club sat at the back half, and no doubt I'll find her there. I spot her and immediately know that she's the *principessa*, laughing and drinking at a circular table, two women by her side. Her smile is radiant, and the brown curls were pinned into a perfect ensemble at the back of her head. Bright green eyes sparkle in the candlelight of the room and red tints cover her cheeks, probably from her drink.

As I step closer and closer to her, I can hear her giggling with the two women at her side. Just as I am about to call her name, a hand on my shoulder stops me. "Private area, no entry without invitation."

He's one of hers. I can see it in how he's put himself between me and her. But I'm taller, and over his shoulder I can see her eyes trained on his, watching how the encounter will end. Will he throw me out? Will I turn around and leave? There is a sense of panic in her eyes, she's scared, which is strange because she doesn't know me. She shouldn't be expecting me, and we've never met so she shouldn't recognize me.

"I'm not gonna hurt your boss," I tell him, letting him know that I know exactly who and what she is. "Just want to talk to her."

"Yeah? And who are you?"

I lean in close to whisper in his ear, "*Sono il suo capo. Fammi passare o avremo un problema serio.*" I grab his shoulders, easily moving him to the side. She's staring at me now, looking at me up and down. Curiosity gleams as I approach her, a question on her lips on how I got past her big bad bodyguard. "Miss Sanna."

"It seems I am at a disadvantage as I don't know you," she stands, walking around the table to put nothing between us.

"Oh, it's not important," I reply, holding out my hand. She takes it slowly, as if she is going to shake it. My impulses take over, and I ask her, "Can we dance?" The words leave me before I can even think. This woman, this *capo*, has plagued my thoughts for three years. She's been my personal obsession – fed by her second and maid. Now that she's in front of me, a vision of beauty, grace, and pure mafia power, I want a taste. A touch. Something that I know will only further my addiction.

"We can if you tell me your name," she negotiates, her smirk captivating me. Yet in her eyes I see the hesitation. She hides it well, the fear. But as she looks me up and down, I see her assessing if I'm a threat, but I'm not ready to clue her in on the situation quite yet.

I decide to start towards the dance floor, and as I had assumed, she follows me. A new song begins, and I place my hand on her waist.

She's warm and soft. All feminine hips and curves. When her hands touch me – fire burns through my skin and straight to my cock. I fight every urge that demands I pull her closer. She's a lady, and even if I know her... she doesn't know me.

We keep a slow pace, spinning around with the other couples on the floor. Her eyes avoid mine, instead glancing at all of the guards posted around the room. They seem unsure, watching me closely with her. Someone got too close to her recently, that much is clear. She had a close encounter with a rival, and they are watching her back more closely as a response. They're loyal, protective. That's good. She'll need that.

"So will you tell me?" Miss Sanna asks about halfway through the song. I've enjoyed watching her too much to think about how to tell her I'm a Bendoni. If I was checking in on any other family this way it would be a sign of disrespect, there is no doubt in my mind she will take it the same way.

The one I'd spoken too whispers in the ear of another. Word is spreading that the boss's boss is in the room. All her men's eyes train on us. They're fixated on her and me, watching to see if I make the wrong move. "How long would it take them to kill me if you gave the word?"

"I beg your pardon?"

"What's the sign? Do I have to threaten you first?"

"Are you threatening me?" Her arms tense and her hips start to move away from me, but I hold her firm.

"No." I tighten my grip on her, keeping her close so I don't have to raise my voice. "I'm just curious. How long would it take them? You have a lot of them in tonight, are you feeling particularly threatened this evening?"

"Who are you?" she isn't flirting anymore; her voice is harsh. Miss Sanna is done letting me play with her. It is a sad turn of events; our lovely moment has come to an end.

"If I told you, we won't be dancing." The song ends and she pulls her hand from mine, escaping from my hold. I sigh, knowing it is over anyway, "My name is Noè Bendoni, from the New York Bendoni's. Is there somewhere we can talk in private?"

I feel it in my spine this time when she looks me up and down, assessing me and the danger I pose. Then she nods, her hand up and waving at one of the girls. "Follow me," she says before leading me through the room and to a back staircase. Up we go, with one of the girls following behind me and then a fourth set of feet are coming up the stairs, one of her goons.

She takes me into a dark office, turning on lamps in the room before sitting behind the large desk. The girl and goon go to stand behind her, both watching me. Ledgers are stacked on a bookshelf behind her, obviously part of the Sanna family's success is their ability to record. Yet, even with all their records and incriminating evidence that sat behind her, the cops have only interfered with their operations a handful of times.

"Please sit, Mr. Bendoni," she gestures to the couch behind me. I take the place she's assigned me. The girl's eyes widen as Miss Sanna revealed my name, no doubt as surprised at my presence as the boss lady herself. "What can I do for you?"

"My father sent me to check in, we heard about your run in with the cops and a possibility of a rat in your circle," I explain to her, making myself comfortable on the couch. My left leg crosses over my right and I fold my hands in my lap.

"We are dealing with it," she tells me snippily. Exactly as I predicted, she's offended by my presence.

"He also wanted to extend a personal invitation to New York in May," I add, knowing it pisses my padre off that she doesn't come. "He urged you to accept."

Miss Sanna gives me a playful smile, "I've heard of the things you do, but I never thought you'd be his mouthpiece. A good little boy you are coming here to tell me all that personally."

I clench my hands together, my eyebrow twitching at her insinuation, "I wanted to come."

"I'm sure this was all your idea." Her smile both irritates and intrigues me. She's goading me, playing with me as payback for earlier. I almost want to laugh. Coming from her... I almost enjoy it.

"Why all the security tonight? More cops?"

"We had some issues earlier, but it's been

dealt with." Her chin tilts down and she looks at me through her lashes. A lesser man would be scared. Instead of fear, the thought of going to her and touching her smooth skin pulses through my mind. To kiss her and feel those lashes flutter against my cheek.

"Tell me."

"Is that an order, boss?" Her tone teeters on disrespect, and I fight my smile.

A tone that would make me want to see another man bleed, on her, makes my heart race and calls to the basic male urges inside me. "Consider it one, yes." And just like that, the idea of ordering her around is very *very* intriguing.

"I believe you are familiar with my cousin?"

"I am."

"He decided to take some shots at me earlier and my boys can be a little paranoid when it comes to my safety. Most are here voluntarily." Interesting. They are giving up a Friday night by their own volition to make sure she is safe. Not the kind of loyalty the other mafia bosses inspire.

"Is he dead?"

"Not yet," she bites out.

"And your *verme*?"

"We are still investigating."

"You should probably find him before the new club opens."

"I'm not stupid," she says as though she's reminding me. Her tone has taken a turn I do not appreciate. It instantly puts a bucket of water on the fire that was burning in my chest for her. She's gone too far. If it were any other boss, I would be encouraging him to remember his place.

"Don't confuse my niceties, Miss Sanna. I will be respected."

"And I ask the same."

"I have been respectful."

"You come unannounced, you speak to me under false pretenses, and you imply I am ill-equipped to do my job," she lists my perceived transgressions. "I'd say you've been anything but respectful."

"I only want to help."

"I don't want your help."

"Yet you've had it for three years," I tell her, standing from my seat. "You think my father's left you alone for three years because of what, your name? No. If Cristiano wasn't such a *piccola puttana* then he would be in your place right now. It was me that convinced him to give you a chance, me and your Di Pietro. You have done well, I will give you that victory, but do not think for a minute you won it alone. You want my respect, you have it. I however will not sit here and let you act as though you are above me, Miss Sanna."

"I own Chicago."

"Your future husband owns Chicago, and you are merely here in the interim," I remind her, probably harsher than needed. I need to remind myself as well, she needs to get married, and it will be her husband that rules this city. The thought of that hypothetical man makes me take a growling tone with her, "And in case you needed a reminder on how the mafia works, you've missed some curtsies. I am above you, while I'm here, I *own* Chicago. You may think this throne is yours, but it is not."

"My apologies," her jaw ticks as she stands. "Mr. Bendoni, Chicago is yours."

CHAPTER 10

Adelaide Sanna

"I might actually kill him," I tell Irene once we got to my house. "My own hands strangling his neck and watching the life drain from him."

"I know you're mad--"

"That is an understatement, Irene." I rip off my shoes and gloves, wanting to get rid of the entire outfit since he touched me in it. That man is infuriating. First, he flirts and dances with me and then he's a total douchebag. What kind of psychotic, egotistical, son of a--

"Are you alright, ma'am?" Beth asks me from the dining room. She comes into the foyer with concern lacing in her features.

"I'm alright, Beth," I grumble.

"A Bendoni boy is here," Irene explains to her. "Expect a bad mood for a few weeks."

"He would never have come it I were a man," I point out, pouring myself a drink.

"But you are not," Irene responds, sitting in

the chair by the fireplace. "And you refuse to get married."

She's been as bad as her father on that topic since she let Doriano take her to the altar a year and a half ago. Everyone knows I will marry eventually; it will become increasingly important once Nonno dies. As much as I hate it, there are just certain things I can't do as a woman.

Still, I scoff at Irene, "Well, your father has been pushing that man on me for three years and I'm glad I never gave in. If we were married, I'd have killed him already."

"I can't believe you didn't invite him to stay at the house."

"Have you heard anything I've said, Irene? I would rather die."

"It is proper to have him stay here. He is your boss."

"Don't remind me of that tragedy. To think he feels entitled to Chicago!"

"He is entitled to Chicago. He is entitled to every city on this continent. That man you're threatening is Bettino Bendoni's *son*, that means he is a *principe* of this country, of the whole damn mafia. He gets what he wants, and I'd recommend that you give it to him. The sooner he is pleased the sooner he will leave."

I take a deep breath, willing myself to calm down. She is right, I just need to suffer through a week or so with him and he will leave. This will all be over soon, and I can get back to my life. He may be a *principe* but I'm the *regina* of this city and no one will change that. Not even a Bendoni.

"You're right. Ask him to breakfast tomorrow with me, I will invite him to stay here while he is in town. He obviously wants me to be angry, and to see all my weak points. We will show him our Chicago has no weaknesses."

He is ten minutes late. I sent word to him last night to meet me at this cafe for breakfast at eight o'clock and he is ten minutes late. All I can do is wait. There is no room for me to get angry at him today, I have to be civil to convince him to leave. This man will not get a rise out of me; he will not create a reaction I don't even have towards Cristiano.

Thinking of my cousin sends a shiver down my spine, he was in the wind and the men who helped him at the warehouse were ghosts. We can't seem to find where they are from or who they really work for. Cristiano obviously hired them, but we do know they aren't from Chicago, my men would know if we were dealing with an internal threat.

Eleven minutes, and he strides in with all the arrogant confidence of a *principe*. It boils my blood. "Good morning, Miss Sanna."

"Mr. Bendoni," I greet him, standing as he takes a seat at the table I've gotten for us. I sit after him, and by the pleased look on his face, he knows

I've been waiting. "I thought we could have a civil conversation, just the two of us."

"Four of your men are in this cafe. One at the bar over there, two at that table, and one outside the door. I am not stupid, Miss Sanna, we are not alone." He smirks, satisfied with his observation.

"They volunteered to come, they want to see how you work," I explain to him. I gave each of my guards the chance to have the day off, all refused. They'd never met a Bendoni before and just as they assessed me in my first few months as their boss, they will also assess him. He owns Chicago while he's here, this is the price that comes with it.

"I'd assume not much differently than you. Although I hear you pin your kills on the Irish." His eyes narrow on me, waiting got my reaction.

"It's good business practice to never have the police looking too closely at my boys," I reply with a confident smirk. I play dirty, but I do it to protect my own. "I hear you leave yours dangling in front of cops' front doors."

"I like to make a show."

"That's apparent," I tilt my head, treating him as I would any other threat. Most of the police or opposing criminals that go up against me fall to me because I'm a woman. They see me as non-threating. I hope putting up my nice young lady act for him will get him gone quicker.

He frowns. "Don't do that."

"Do what?" I smirk.

"Play with me," his voice drops and my heart

jumps. My heart jumps? Is that fear? No, no I fear nothing. I haven't felt fear since I threw Crisitano out of Chicago three years ago. I froze myself off to fear when I became a mafia boss. I've seen too much in my life to be afraid of one man. Especially not this man.

"I'm not playing."

"That's a lie," he smiles then. "You're lying to me. I don't like that."

"I'm not lying. I'm not playing."

His hand reaches out and grabs mine, "I can't help you if you're playing with me, *principessa*."

"*Regina*," I correct him. "I am no princess. I am a queen. This is my kingdom and if you think for a second, I'll let you take my throne, we will have a problem."

He chuckled at my words, leaning back into his seat. "I'm not here for your throne, *regina*. I won't take anything from you unless you ask me too. I just want to help."

"I don't need help," I remind him. "I've done this for three years."

"I know," his voice is softer, and so are his eyes. Everything seems to soften, like he has given up fighting with me. "However, there are concerns coming from New York. No one thought you'd be doing this for three years."

"Your father thought I'd be married by now and a pre-approved mafia lord would be on my throne," I say for him, reading the unspoken words on his lips.

He sighs, "Yes."

I look away from him, not able to stand the intensity of his gaze. My two men sitting at another table check in with me, and I give them a small nod, telling them I'm alright. Di Pietro has pushed me to get married for years, so have a few of the others. For my own security mostly, they know a woman is vulnerable to scrutiny and attacks. Like the one Cristiano launched against me recently. He would give up once I wed, that's the hope anyway.

Yet, marrying a man simply for security feels like a betrayal to my younger self. I grew up around Auntie Ellen and Uncle David, a perfect pair. They complimented each other so well, sometimes I wondered if getting married made you able to read your partner's mind with the way they acted. They were so in sync with each other and always willing to meet the needs and expectations of the family. I want that in a husband, someone who I understand and who understands me. Those mafia lords on Di Pietro's list would marry me with few questions, because I hold the keys to Chicago. I never wanted that.

"I will marry someday," I finally say to him.

"When?"

"When I find a man I can trust."

CHAPTER 11

Noè Bendoni

Miss Sanna allowed me to go with her on all her business for the day. That included going to the warehouse where she'd been shot at the night before. Her cousin, Cristiano Sanna, was posing a threat with a greater magnitude than she understood. What she doesn't know is the boy has sent numerous letters to me, Elio, and padre over the years expressing contempt with how she's run the city. He's a traitor and she hasn't realized it yet. That's what makes him dangerous, he's her family and she's blind to it.

I watch her conduct business, standing behind her as she directs the workers where each case will be delivered too. She has the clubs equally supplied, but it is obvious the booze meets the cliental. *Claudia* gets more high-end booze, mainly liquors and wines. While the clubs have cheaper products, she's also supplying liquor to those venues, it isn't bourbon or fine vodka. It's moonshine mostly from the south, and beer made locally in Illinois.

She checks on each location later, making sure they are well stocked for the month, checking ledgers, speaking to her managers, and walking the buildings.

We end our afternoon at her new club, the one raided by police recently. Renovations were nearing completion on the interior and with a fully stocked bar and bands booked for two months, she was ready to open this Friday night. A staff full of woman manned the club, ready to serve and sell all the illegal contraband that Miss Sanna peddles. It was impressive, to say the least. One of the construction workers told me the building had been abandoned for ten years before Miss Sanna bought it in her grandfather's name. The club had a gold and grey theme, with blue accents across the dance floor and stage. She's made the place her own, and it is very different from the ones built by her father and grandfather.

"It is nice," I compliment her once she's done conversing with her staff.

"It is the second one I've built. My grandfather built three, my father built three, and my goal is to add three as well for my children to inherit."

"You need to get married first," I remind her, knowing her marriage would get my padre off my ass about her running Chicago.

"Is that a proposal?" she jokes, busying her hands with paperwork.

"Do you want it to be?"

Her eyes shoot to mine and her body goes stiff before she answers, "No."

"Then it isn't a proposal."

"You intrigue me, Noè Bendoni." When she says my name, my chest tightens, and I have to take a deep breath to lessen the pressue. It doesn't work completely; the tightness is still there, and it worsens the longer I stare into her moss green eyes.

"How so?"

"You're not exactly what I expected of a *principe*. I mean, you are arrogant and selfish, but you are also kind to me. Kinder than I assume you are to the other bosses."

"You're not like the other bosses, you're a woman."

She huffs, "Is that all? You're not impressed at all?"

"I'm impressed because you're a woman." She turns her back to me, walking the length of the bar to pass off her paperwork to one of her female employees. When she comes back, she does it with a smile and a glint of darkness in her eyes.

"You may be impressed because I'm a woman, but we both know you came because your curiosity of me was piqued. Three years and I've had one run in with the police. How have I done it when other bosses face criminal charges on a month-to-month basis? Three years and I've built two clubs when women can't own property. Three years and I've single handedly started the gun trade in this city. You're impressed because I'm a woman running this city better than half your other bosses run theirs."

"I won't deny your successes, but the truth of the matter is, you cannot do this forever. My padre won't let you do this forever."

"I don't need forever, I just need time," she says with finality before changing the subject. "My father is probably rolling in his grave knowing I haven't invited you into our home. Where are you staying?"

"Over on Ohio Street."

"Come stay with me while you're here. It is the least I can do."

"I thought you'd never ask," I say with a smirk. "It is only courteous."

Miss Sanna took me home, feeding me at her table with her grandfather. Padre used to tell me stories of Lucilio Sanna and how he took Chicago from the hands of the Irish in the name of the Italian mafia. To see him this way, a fragile old man who remembers little and understand less, it makes me tremble.

My own grandfathers died long before this point, the life of a mafia boss leave few to retire and grow old. Yet here he was, an old man with no one left but a granddaughter to care for him and a grandson to disappoint him. His three children are gone, and three of his grandchildren. With Cristano having avoided Chicago for three years, the woman sitting across from him is truly all he has in this world. A girl that he barely saw growing up and an old man she hardly knew, yet she took it upon herself to care for his health and his legacy.

It is more than the fact that she is a woman that impresses me, not many women would do what she's done. Her life is on the line every day for men she hardly knew, for men that shipped her downstate for most of her childhood. When her family needed her most, she returned and learned the politics of mafia life to uphold what Lucilio created. Not many women I knew would've done what she's done. If I'd been in her shoes, what would I have done?

Probably handed it off to Cristiano and returned downstate, to a life I knew. It is what everyone expected of her. Yet here she is, defying all those expectations by putting in the work not many men I know would have done.

She is impressive in a way I didn't think was possible.

"Mr. Bendoni?" she calls, pulling me from my thoughts and back to her and the meal placed in front of me.

"My apologies, I was collecting wool."

"Do you want to go with me then?"

"Go with you where?"

"You really weren't listening?"

"I apologies greatly for that."

"It is Saturday, I usually go to one of the clubs on Saturdays. Do you want to accompany me to one of the clubs?"

"Yes," I give her a warm smile. "I would like that a lot."

An hour later, we found ourselves changed into evening clothing and driving to one of her clubs. She has passed me the keys to one of her father's cars, saying her guards would be meeting us there. The drive was short and silent for the most part. The hum of the car being the loudest noise as we went several blocks to her club. By the time we arrived, people were already lined the streets of one of the clubs built by her father. We parked down the block, and she took my arm as we walked up to the club.

"Good evening, boss," the doorman greats while opening the door for us.

"Thank you, Freddie. Have we been busy?"

"Normal from what I've seen."

"Good," she calls back as we enter the club. The band was loud, and jazz music filled the buildings. Circular tables lined the room while the center was open for dancing, and people were dancing. Bodies lined the room, and the smell of smoke and booze filled the air.

Miss Sanna leads me to the bar and orders us both drinks. I'm still surveying the club, checking to see how many of her men *volunteered* to be here tonight. She passes me a drink, and I sip on the burning liquor before facing her.

"You're looking for my boys?"

"I am."

"Oh, they don't know where I am yet. Freddie saw me so word will spread, and they'll eventually make their way here. You have a total of ten minutes with me alone." My heart skips at beat as she smiles wickedly at me. Like she knows exactly what she does to me with that look. "Let's dance."

CHAPTER 12

Noè Bendoni

This sirena took my hand and drug me to the middle of the dance floor. The song changed and she began to dance with me. Bodies surrounded us, pushing us closer together. Her hand slips into mine as we start the fast-paced dance. I spin her around and a smile grows, lifting her cheeks. It isn't her fake smile, the one I see when she tries to play me. It isn't the nervous smile from when we first met yesterday, and she didn't know me. It is her real smile.

The smile of a lady enjoying my company.

We dance and spin and fall into each other as others around us move back and forth. I catch her close in my arms when a woman behind her pushes her into me. We laugh. I get a genuine part of her for ten minutes, and then through the back room, two men emerge, and I know my time is up.

Di Pietro being one of those men.

I escort her back off the floor, leaving her in the care of one of her friends before making my way to Di Pietro.

"Where are you going?" she asks as I start to walk away.

"I have some business with your second," I tell her, my hand itching to tuck one of her curls behind her ears. "We had a good ten minutes, but I have business here as much as you do."

Her smile falls and her expression turns cold once more, I've lost her. She nods and gestures for me to leave, so I do. I find the man who's played a main part in my obsession with her. "Di Pietro," I grumble, shaking his hand.

"Bendoni," he greets. "Let's take this somewhere private."

He takes me down a back hall and into a small office. It was very different from the one at *Claudia.* This one was simpler, the wooden furniture cheaper and the seats made of cloth instead of leather. An office for a club manager, not Miss Sanna. I sit in one of those cloth chairs and instead of behind the desk, Di Pietro joins me on the other.

"She's different than you described."

"She is who she is," he replies shortly. "Why are you here?"

"Padre was concerned about the police interference. We've seen more and more of it recently and he didn't like that they searched her new club."

"Is that all?"

"No. He was also pissed that she's never

shown her face in New York. There is a lot about Miss Sanna he doesn't know so he sent me to check in on her. I'll admit I had a few curiosities of my own, after all your letters."

He chuckles, sitting tall in his seat, "Your father wants to see her married and someone else take over."

"He does, but when I return, I'll tell him that all is well and there is no need to push the subject."

"You would do that?" his asks while raising his eyebrow in suspicion.

"Yes." I might just do anything for her. This is a simple task. Helping her with my father and buying her time to find a man she trusts is the least I can do.

"You're a good man. I wish she'd listen to me about you."

What has he told her about me? Suddenly, I'm filled with worry and curiosity. He feeds me information on her, but what does he tell her about me? Is it good? Does he tell her all I've done and worked for in New York, or just all the monstrous acts I do as one of my padre's enforcers? As if on instinct, I need to know who she thinks I am. I need to know what she thinks of me. Who am I in her world?

So, I ask, "What have you told her?"

"I've told her it should be you she marries. I've put you on the top of her lists."

Lists. A practice we've done for our girls since our creation. A list of approved boys within the mafia fit to marry them. Every father did it for their daughter. Sometimes grandfathers or uncles would contribute. I'd know her father put me on his list, hell, he wanted to set it up himself to ensure I'd marry her. Yet, when I heard he died without making our introduction, I backed down, not wanting to show up and tell her that marrying me had been his wish. Knowing her now, I doubt she'd have listened.

"You didn't tell me that."

"You didn't need to know."

We sit in silence, that is until I bring up an important change of subjects. "Have you found Cristiano?"

"Not yet, I'm sure the snake will rear his head at the club opening this Friday."

"You should probably kill him before that."

Di Pietro sighs, "It isn't that simple. A kill like that, boss will want to be present, and I don't know if she can watch him die."

"She's seen death before."

He gave a nervous chuckle, "She's killed before. This is different though, this is blood. Her blood. It will be hard for her."

"Discussing me behind my back," she says from the doorway. I hadn't heard her come back, neither had Di Pietro from the look on his face. The music from the band vibrated off the walls, which had drowned out her footsteps. She knew we were back here discussing her life and business. "Crisitano is a traitor, I know that now. The fact that neither of you trust me to know that reflects on your own idiocrasy, not my naivety."

"Boss--"

"Quit while you're ahead, Di Pietro," Miss Sanna warns him.

"Mr. Bendoni had some questions."

"Questions he should have asked me," she turns to glare at me this time. We've both angered her, and the look in her eyes burns my stomach. "You've been informing on me. Tattling to the head family my business."

"It isn't like that," I jump in, standing to put myself between Miss Sanna and Di Pietro.

She puts her hand up to stop me, tilting her head as she asks, "So, what is it like?" Her words bite, her tone laced with venom.

I stand silent, trying to think of my next words. She is the boss here and she feels betrayed by Di Pietro's correspondence with me. The wrong words could land the gentleman dead and while she cannot kill me without facing padre's wrath, having one of her men take a finger or too wouldn't be seen as overly excessive. Her eyebrow rises, waiting for my explanation and I swallow at the murder in her eyes. Not much scares me, certainly not any of the city leaders across this country, but that look has me wanting to tuck my tail and run. Like anything I say will be wrong and leave us in a worst position than we are in now.

"I'm waiting."

"I know."

"I hate waiting."

"I gathered that this morning." I smirk; her scowl deepens; I stop smirking.

"You're stalling."

"I am," I reply honestly. "Di Pietro can we have the room?"

"No, I should stay."

"You should leave," Miss Sanna corrects him, giving him the same murderous look she's been giving me. He nods, stands, and leaves. She closes the door behind him. "You have my attention, as always."

"Two days and it's 'always' already."

"You have proven to be a stick in my side for two days."

"Di Pietro sent me information on you on my orders, he was doing my bidding," I tell her, stepping forwards and taking one of her gloved hands. "He never betrayed you, he never would from what I can tell. Your men are yours and I highly doubt anything I or my padre could do will ever change that."

"Why?"

"Why what?"

"Why spy on me? Was it because you didn't trust me?"

"It wasn't that. I was just curious."

"That's a poor excuse."

"It is true." We are close, both of us having inched more and more as we spoke. I place her hand on my chest, letting her feel my heartbeat. "It wasn't that I didn't trust you, I was intrigued by you. I wanted to know everything about you and how you ran this city. I learned very quickly the kind of woman you are, and it had me obsessed. His letters fueled my obsession with you. I never shared the information I had, never let his letters be used against you. My padre sent me here because he doesn't trust you, but he sent me instead of my brother because I've defended you for years. I have fought every battle for you in New York.

"He wanted you to give it up, to pass it along to Cristiano. I reminded him of the fool your cousin is, and I told him that we didn't want a man like your cousin running a city for us. Cristiano came to New York seven times in the past years and each time I fought him for you. I protected you from living under him. I did that for you. I warned Di Pietro of the danger you were in with Cristiano, and he told me when you married none of it would matter, that you'd be safe then, but you never did. You are in danger here, and one more mishap with Cristiano might leave you dead or worse... at his mercy.

"So, find a man you can trust, find him sooner rather than later. Your life will change if what happened with him last time happens again."

CHAPTER 13

Adelaide Sanna

I took his words to heart. I thought about them night and day for the next four days. Sunday at mass I was focusing on nothing more than my list. I had memorized many of the names by now, the ones that don't change month to month are rolling over in my head. I'd never met any of them, but one word from me and any of them would come to Chicago to court me. Bendoni sat beside me in mass, his closeness to me only serving to remind me of his warning. His words rang through my mind all of Sunday. That and the feeling of his chest under my hand.

Monday brought with it work at the docks, and he came with me. Every piece of business I had, he stood behind me as I cared for it. Only when Irene and I sat in my study at the house was I really out of his presence, and even then, I could see him out the window, reading to Nonno on the front porch.

"We have two incoming shipments from

downstate coming in by train on Wednesday, and a load of military-line guns coming by ship on Friday morning. Renzi says he can handle the distribution on Wednesday without you but requests your presence on Friday morning. Titone will be there as well, it is a large shipment," Irene rattles off. I know I'm supposed to be listening, but I can't stop staring at Bendoni speaking in fluent Italian.

"Tell them I'll be there in the morning when the boat comes in," I say, but my distraction is obvious. Irene closes her folder she was reading though and set it on my desk. The loud smack of the leather on wood makes me jump.

"Are you still planning on killing him?" she asks me seriously. After a beat of staring at one another we both break out laughing.

"Not anymore, I guess. You know your father was reporting on me to him for the past three years?" I ask her, still recovering from our fit of laughter.

"What? I had no idea. What are you going to do to him?"

I shake my head, "Nothing. From what Bendoni said, he ordered it. He said your father's letters made him *obsessed* with me."

"Obsessed?" Irene gives me a joking grin. "Obsessed enough to call on you properly?"

I roll my eyes, "Please, he's as interested in courting me as you are in having your nails ripped from your fingers." Irene shutters, she watched it happen once and lost her lunch seconds after.

"I don't know," she draws out after she finishes cringing. "Obsessed sounds like interest to me. How long did my father write to him."

"Three years."

"That's a long obsession."

I clear my throat, my chest tightening at her insinuation. I take the file and open it, finding the details on the gun shipment coming in. "The guns, they're from where again?"

"Trickle down from New York, they couldn't push the product in New York so they distributed them across the country."

"Okay, and tell Renzi I will be there on Wednesday," I look out to Bendoni again. Nonno is smiling at him. I feel my own obsession growing. He said he is staying until the club opened on Friday, but sometime in me said that come next Monday he would still be here with no plans of leaving. Still, I held onto the idea that he would be leaving this weekend. His presence only fueled this new obsession.

Tuesday went by uneventfully, I spent most of my day at *Petit Coeur,* putting on finishing touches for the grand opening on Friday. He waited for me in the corner, looking over each detail of my club and nodding to each in approval.

Wednesday, he sat with me as Father David spoke with Nonno and gave him communion. After his small, personal service with Nonno, I walked the Father out of the house. He stops at the gate, turning to me before he leaves.

"Have you spoken to him about his wishes, after he passes?"

"He will be buried with my Nonna, next to my father, mother, and brother."

He gave a small smile, "His time is coming quick, it is best we start preparing for a time without him in this world."

I give him an understanding nod before sending him away. Before I can turn back into the house, I see Bendoni standing in the doorway. He steps down the stoop and sat on the porch furniture. His eyes gleam with sympathy as he stares up at me from his seat.

"Don't look at me that way," I warn him, sitting at his side. "I've known for three years that he is dying. He's old, and when people get old, they die."

"You will be alone." The hurt in his voice is clear, and it pains me more to see his eyes look at me that way than to know Nonno is dying. His pity is evident in those eyes. For most of our people, family is the foundation. Everything a mafia man does; he does for his wife and children. We care for our family in the Italian mafia, that's why despite not knowing Nonno for most of my life, I've cared for him as any Italian granddaughter would for their Nonno.

"Not true, I'm sure Cristiano will be alive," I joke, chuckling at myself. I laugh more at the dark look in his eyes.

"Don't joke about that."

"Sorry," I say, leaning back into my chair to be in an unlady-like position. "It will be strange to live in this house alone."

"Beth won't stay?"

"She will have no need too. I don't need a full-time caregiver. I will make sure she finds a good position in another house though," I explain to him. Beth will get a glowing recommendation from me, and Mary will stay as my maid as I have no interest in cleaning the house on a regular basis.

"Well, you'll find you man who you can trust and not be alone," he says as he stands. He looks down on me then, his eyes soft and almost hopeful. "What else is on the addenda for the day?"

"Warehouses by the trainyard, I have a shipment from Vinegar Hill coming in,"

"Vinegar Hill?"

"It's downstate, not the real name of the town but it's what the boxes are labeled as," I reply, standing to meet him. "Are you coming?"

"Always."

"Five days and it is now 'always?'"

"I enjoy being a stick in your side."

Thursday came and went and soon enough it is Friday. I spend all day Friday at the club, making sure everything is perfect. Mr. Bendoni stayed home all day, leaving me to work, which I was grateful to him for doing. When he follows me all day, I can't focus properly. It is like my eyes are always searching for him, my body ready to feel his warmth nearby. He stayed away though and I got a significant amount of work done. It isn't until dinner that I return home, and hope Beth made something. I usually cook for us, but I don't make it home until six-thirty and have no desire to make a meal after the long day.

"Good evening," Bendoni greets me as I walk into the door. He stands in the doorway to the dining room, a large smile on my face.

"Good evening," I say back cautiously. I take off my shoes and gloves before walking towards him. The scene seems unreal, as though he isn't really here. Or this isn't really him. The smell of dinner hits me before he steps into the room and gives me a view of the table. Roasted duck, fried potatoes, beans, fresh bread, and a pudding sit on the table, the smell of the meal radiates in the dining room. Beth and Nonno sit at the table, obviously waiting for me to eat. "What is this?"

"Dinner," Bendoni replies as he moves around me to pull out a chair. "Come sit."

I sit, watching as he moves to sit beside me, as we have every night since he came to stay here. Nonno was always wheeled to the head of the table, and Beth and I always sat beside him to help in the eating process.

"Did you make this?" I ask Beth. She's never

been much of a cook so seeing the spread I am surprised by the effort. When I'm home too late to cook we usually have beans and ham or canned soups. Rice and chicken when she reals adventurous. This, this is a full and proper meal that I know she is incapable of cooking. So, when she shakes her head, I turn to Bendoni. "Who did you pay to cook this?"

He chuckles at me, "No one. I paid no one. I made it myself."

"You can cook?"

"Don't act so surprised, there is a lot about me you don't know."

"Obviously."

He carves the duck, serving each of us before himself as we all eat together. He and Beth catch me up on the happenings of the day. Apparently Nonno got enough clarity to tell them about his wedding day in *Italia* and my father's birth in this house. I'm sad I missed it, but glad Bendoni was here to understand his Italian to tell me about it. Beth only knows bits and pieces of the language she's picked up through the years, and often when he's speaking, she cannot understand him. Knowing Bendoni was here to learn so much about him, it makes me happy.

After dinner, Beth takes Nonno to get cleaned up for bed while I start with dishes. Then, I prepare to open the club. I dress in a dark purple dress, with black gloves and a glittering headpiece with shining diamonds across my forehead. After

I finish some makeup and make sure my curls are still presentable, I head downstairs.

Bendoni waits by the fireplace, dressed in a sharp black suit with a tie of dark purple that matches my dress. I stop at the last step, taking him in. Something changed between the first time I saw him and now. When he first told me his name, I felt small. He made me feel small after three years of being the boss around here. It angered me. Now, standing in front of him, I no longer felt small. Like in the short week together, he let me grow and be who I am around him. He didn't correct me or even try to control my decisions regarding Chicago's mafia. He trusted me to do what I've done for three years, and that means something to me.

My skin buzzes as he walks up to me, he stands across from me, only the banister between us. I reach out, fixing his tie so it is straight down his chest, but my hands rest there. I want to touch him, to feel his heartbeat and his chest expanding with his breath. It comforts me in a way I've never known comfort.

"If Cristiano comes tonight, I will kill him myself," I tell him, our eyes meeting as my hands stay planted on his chest.

"I know." His own hand moves slowly, as if waiting for my permission, before resting on my cheek. "You look beautiful, Adelaide."

"Thank you, Noè."

Something has changed, and I like what has

become of us.

CHAPTER 14

Noè Bendoni

I drive us to Petit Coeur and find the whole block filled with people waiting to get into the club. Tonight will be a success and I'm glad I will get to witness it. I park us next to the club; a spot being left open for her arrival. We both exit the car, and she puts her arm in the crook of mine as we walk to the front entrance. The crowd roars and cheers, knowing she is here to open the club. One of the men places a box on the ground and I help her up onto it so the crowd can better see her.

"Thank you all for joining me tonight," she yells over the block full of people. "I am so happy to see so many familiar faces in the crowd. We have worked hard to turn this old place into what I'm presenting you with today. I want to thank all the workers here tonight and all those that have helped make this place what it is. We have a great band tonight, so please come in and enjoy."

The doors opened and Adelaide leads us inside, the band started playing and it only took a minute before the crowd consumed the club. Alcohol was being poured, couples mingled on the dance floor, and a buzz overcame the room of conversation and laughter. Adelaide watched it all from a corner table that she and I share. She just wants to watch it all, that's what she said on the drive over. At her first club opening, she'd been too stressed to remember it all, but this time she would savor it. So, I sat with her, watching the success that rained over the building.

A server brings us champagne, a sweet bubbly mix, which I lift to toast, "To you, Adelaide Sanna, the only female mafia boss in history and to the legacy you have created." We cheer our glasses before each taking a sip.

"When will you leave?" she asks. Adelaide turns her attention fully to me, shifting her body to face me instead of the club before her. She has her win for the year, the opening of this club will shine on her for months to come, yet that look in her eyes, the twitching of her fingers, makes me wonder if there is another prize she's after.

"Do you want me gone?" If she tells me to go, I will. I will happily leave for New York on the next train and report to my padre the honest truth: she is the most capable mafia boss I know. But if she asks me to stay...

"Give me ten minutes," she says, standing and offering me her hand.

"Why, Miss Sanna, are you asking me to dance?"

"Adelaide," she corrects me immediately. "Addy."

I rise from my seat, standing several inches above her. "Alright, Addy, ten minutes."

She takes me to the floor that can hardly hold two more bodies, but we find space. I take her hand, spinning her around before pulling her into my chest. She smiles and the crowd fades. It is just us dancing on this floor, even the music starts to fade. My sole focus is on her, watching her move and how her dress flows around her hips.

The purple fabric mesmerizes me, moving with her and showing off the subtle curves of her body. Dancing seemed to be the place she is honest with me, the place she finds herself most relaxed.

Addy grabs my hands, pulling me to dance closer to her, "Don't slow down on me, I have you for ten minutes." I give her one of my real smiles, ones I don't use often but I've found myself always giving her. She deserves my real smile.

Our ten minutes on the dance floor ended with shots at the bar, drinking with some of her men that worked on the construction that she had personally invited tonight. We drink and dance for much longer than ten minutes. We laughed and let liquor warm our bellies. Addy relaxed and let herself forget her worries from earlier in the day. Her club is a success, and the relief of that is shown over her face.

Her secretary and Di Pietro came later that night with their spouses in tow. The girl hugs

Addy and congratulates her on the club. Di Pietro had the bartender bring drinks for each of us, even though he could tell Addy and I had been drinking for most of the night. We toast, we drink, and we chat. Di Pietro keeps business talk to a minimum as his wife glares at him when he brings it up.

"This is a party, love," she told him the first time he asked about potential first-night profits. "Enjoy it."

"Yes, Di Pietro, enjoy it," Addy giggles and Irene follows. The two girls are close friends, I see now. We sit and drink and talk and dance. Irene and Mrs. Di Pietro have the second wrapped around their fingers. He is a softer man around them.

After what seemed like hours with Addy and her mafia family, Di Pietro excuses himself for a cigarette, I follow as does his son in law. We take the back door and go into the alley, escaping the noise of the club and leaving the ladies to themselves. Myself and the son-in-law I now know as Doriano, bum cigarettes from Di Pietro and each get a light from him as well.

"No sign of Crisitano," Di Pietro says only after his first drawl of the cigarette.

"None yet, maybe he's smarter than we thought."

"I doubt it," the older man replies. Doriano doesn't speak, he hasn't spoken much since he arrived with his wife this evening. A quite man compared to his wife, who has laughed and laughed and laughed with Addy all night.

"She's drank too much," the son-in-law finally speaks, but I can't tell if he's referring to his wife or his boss.

"Are you going to tell her that?" I question, raising my eyebrow at the man.

"No." We three stand in silence as we smoke, flicking ash to the ground. My head spins a little, making me painfully aware of the alcohol I've consumed tonight. Perhaps Addy and I both overdid it. "When will you leave?"

"When she asks me too," is my only answer. I've made no plans to leave Chicago, hoping that Addy doesn't want me to leave. When she asks me too, which I suspect the topic will come up over breakfast tomorrow, I will make my arrangements. Being here has been too fun for me to want to leave, but I will. I will leave when she tells me too. Give her the space and freedom to find whatever it is she's looking for in this life. Being near her is tempting, so tempting that I can't pull away on my own.

"You want to stay?" Di Pietro asks bluntly, almost knowing what my answer will be.

"He's got it bad for our boss," Doriano says in reply for me, anytime he does speak he annoys me. I prefer it when he's silent.

"I'm your boss's boss," I remind him with a frown. He turns his head down and focuses on his cigarette.

"Do you?"

I make direct eye contact with the man that's put himself in the position as Addy's father. He makes her lists. He is trusted by her. Her second. If I were to ask for anyone's blessing about this, it would be his. Although, I know I have her father's approval, and if Addy wants it that's all I really care about. She makes her own way and her own choices, the only blessing I need to stay is hers.

Before I can reply, four guys start down the alley. We all turn to them, watching them stalk towards us. "This is a private alley," I call down to them, but they don't stop.

I crush out my cigarette on the brick wall, ready to pull my gun. The first guy reaches Doriano and slams his head into the same wall. I pull my gun, but a second one, a bigger one than the one who has Doriano, grabs me and punches. My vision dots and at this point I regret all the alcohol Addy and I shared. My vision blurs worse than it should, half due to the impact, half due to the alcohol.

A second punch makes my eyes water and blood trickle down from my nose. I grab him, my reflexes are slow, but they are starting to kick in. I throw my own fist, landing it on the side of his face. The giant of a human being barely flinches. At my side, I see Di Pietro being thrown to the floor by the other two, them kicking him while he's on the ground. Doriano's head bleeds, red marks coloring the brick wall behind him.

My second punch lands on the guy's eye, making him stumble back. I focus, it is hard to think through the blur that is my memory, but I focus on all the years of fighting on New York's streets. While he's blinking away watery eyes from my punch, I advance. My fists burn with the next few hits, and after a fast combination, I have his throat between my hands and his back against a wall.

"Who are you working for?"

His smirk is bloody, his lip busted from one of my hits. "Your boss is dead."

My chest tightened and threatened my own breathing. My heart was racing from the fight, but it almost stops as he mentions Addy.

"Cristiano Sanna, that's who you work for?" I know it's him, but the attacker needs to tell me directly. Behind me, I hear a cry, and I foolishly turn. That's when my ass hits the ground along with my head.

CHAPTER 15

Adelaide Sanna

Irene and I were giggling as we walked the back hallway to find the men. Noè, Di Pietro, and her husband, Doriano, left to smoke and it was time they came back to enjoy the party. As I lead us through the narrow hallways, my head spins slightly from all the drinks I've consumed. I may have overdone it, but today seems special to me, I feel special today. Celebrating with the boys that worked so hard to turn this place around seemed more important than staying sober.

"Your brother really said that?" I laugh as she continues the story about her younger brother, a boy barely twelve, arguing with his mother over him being a man.

"I thought mamma was going to throw him out of the house," Irene laughs with me, her smile shining across her face and reflecting in her eyes.

The sound of a gunshot makes her smile fall and her eyes darken. I turn from her, running down the hallway to the back entrance, two more shots ring out and I run faster. My shoulder slams into the door and I rush into the alley.

Doriano's slumped frame meets me first; his face is bloody along with the wall behind him. Irene pushes past me. At the end of the alley, two men run from the scene and onto the street. The were tall and blonde, obviously assailants of this situation. Two bodies are dead on the ground, neither I recognize as my own men or Cristiano. Next, I look down, Di Pietro lays in front of me, a bullet wound in his belly that covers his white shirt in blood. Irene screams, dropping down to her father and pressing her hands onto his wound. His breathing is shallow, and he wheezes as he gasps for air.

Frozen as my head turns up to the man reaching for me. I push him, hitting his hands as they reach for me. He seizes me, gripping my shoulders and calling my name. My eyes meet his finally and his voice touches my ears.

"Adelaide," he says again, squeezing my shoulders. The fog in my head clears slightly as I see the blood marring his face. I don't feel myself moving, but before I can fully come into the situation my hand is on his cheeks and I'm searching his body for injuries. Is he shot? He's bleeding from his nose, but I look over his chest and stomach to search for any other wounds. "Adelaide, the police are coming."

The faint noise of sirens comes from the street. "Are you okay?"

"Yes," he answers firmly. "The police are coming, and they will search the club. You need to go hide your inventory."

"You're bleeding." My thumb runs over his lips, removing some of the blood from his face.

"Adelaide, listen to me now," he orders, but the daze over me holds strong. He wants me to leave? That's not right. No, we should leave together. He is hurt and I'm completely alright, a bit drunk, but alright. His eyes leave mine and go to someone behind me. Faint sobs come into my ears, but it isn't Irene he addresses. "Luca, clean out the stock. Police are coming. Felix, bring the car around, Di Pietro needs a doctor."

"Noè," I say, bringing his attention back to me.

"I need you to sober up for me," he pleads. He leans forward and rests his forehead on mine. "I'm okay. Di Pietro has been shot. Doriano is badly hurt. Your men need you need now."

I take a deep breath, closing my eyes as the alley starts spinning. "It was Cristiano."

"It was the Irish," Noè corrects me.

I look back up at him. "You're okay."

He smiles, blood coating his teeth, "I'm okay."

I let go of him and he releases me as well. Felix starts down the alley in one of my father's cars. Irene still cries over her father's bleeding body and Doriano starts to moan as he regains consciousness. Felix jumps out of the car and starts towards Di Pietro.

"Irene, step back," I order her, grabbing her arm and pulling her away from her father. "Noè help Felix get him in the car." The two men lift Di Pietro into the vehicle. Noè comes back to me once the older man is in the car.

"Go inside."

"Take Doriano, go home."

"What?" his eyebrows sink together with his question.

"Go home, I will follow soon."

"You're drunk," he reminds me.

"So are you," I add. "Irene, take Doriano home."

Irene grabs her husband, and both get in the back seat of the car with her father. "I don't want to leave you."

"Go anyway."

"No."

"Yes," I order him. I touch his cheek once more, "Go, the cops will start to ask questions, and it is best you're not here."

His eyes flitter over my face before he nods. He leaves with Felix while I go back into the club. People have started to leave, and knowing the Irish mob has ruined this night makes my blood boil. Luca meets me at the door.

"The girls are taking it all down," he tells me. The girls being those that work at the bar. They're taking my alcohol supply down to the basement, where there is a fake wall to hide it behind. Most of my stock is behind that wall, but what was out for tonight will be taken back down.

"It was the Irish," I tell him. "They shot Di Pietro, and I will have my revenge tonight."

"Yes, boss."

"I'll make an announcement to the club that everything is alright, and the evening can continue." I do just that. I stand in front of my club and make the announcement. People cheer and the band continues to play. Dancing continues.

The police arrive and I show them both bodies in the alley. I lie, saying I had no idea what happened or who pulled the trigger. Part of it is the truth, I don't know exactly who pulled the trigger on those two Irish thugs, but I had a pretty good idea as it was the only man still conscious when I got out there. No doubt the two that lay dead on the pavement were bodies made by Noè. I'd knew he killed before; I had heard of his ruthless killings made on behalf of the Bendoni family's operations in New York. This felt different though, seeing his works. I can't name how I'm feeling, but that could be the alcohol.

The police take my statement and take the bodies. I tell them he wasn't a patron of my club, another truth. These men hadn't been inside tonight. No, they came only for the attack. The alley is left with bloodstains, a reminder of what happened this night. Noè wasn't hurt badly, but he didn't really give me the chance to look him over before I sent him away. I know some of this blood is his and it infuriates me.

As Noè said, they come into the club. They interview people and look for witnesses. There are none. The only witnesses were the two men that ran from the scene as Noè started shooting. Still, they ask half the club questions about the sounds they heard. Half the people here are as drunk or more so than I am, but like me they are faking it well. The police don't even go into the basement, after finding no one that saw the shooting, they leave.

Luca comes with me as I get ready to leave as well. "One of the warehouses was hit, a gun shipment was stolen."

"Cristano, he planned this." It may be the Irish as Noè told me, but my cousin is helping them. Or they are helping him. Either way, he stole from me, and the Irish attacked my men at my club. It was unacceptable. They would all pay for the pain this is causing me.

Luca offers to take me home, but I redirect him. Instead, he drives me to the warehouse by the docks. The one Cristiano hit earlier tonight. I don't want to go home yet, or to the Di Pietro's home where I know Felix took the group from the alley. I have business to take care of before I go check on him.

Warehouse workers were cleaning, taking inventory and making a list of everything stolen. I'm informed it was a group, ten in total. Four died in the warehouse, taking two of my own men with them. In addition to my warehouse workers, a group of my enforcers wait for me at the warehouse. "Boys," I greet them as Luca and I walk into the first room.

"Boss," a few of them nod my way.

"Irish attacked tonight at the club in addition to the mess Cristiano created here. Di Pietro has been shot and Doriano was beaten badly," I explain to them, not wanting to mention Noè Bendoni was with them and was left mostly uninjured. "Two of them died in the attack and two escaped. I hear six survived the attack here. I want them all brought to me, and I want their brothers and sons."

Blood for blood. If Di Pietro dies, then so will their family. The man is like my father in many ways, and I will avenge him the was my father was avenged. Blood for blood. Those men will watch their blood die before they follow into the afterlife, may God have mercy on their souls.

"You want them alive?"

"Yes." I want to kill them myself. "I want who gave the order to attack as well. They will all be brought here for me to question. While you are at it, find Cristiano."

"Yes, ma'am," they answer in unison.

CHAPTER 16

Adelaide Sanna

I stand outside the Di Pietro home only after I'm assured that the enforcers will do their job well. I know the boys well, and I know they'll find the attackers. I returned to the club, too, before coming here. The crowd had died, but the club was still packed with bodies. No more alcohol would be sold tonight, to play it safe. Only after I'm sure everything is orderly do I have Luca take me to the Di Pietro's home.

He stands with me now, as I stare at the house with a tremble in my hand. Noè is inside, and what happened in the alley haunts me. I froze. Seeing Noè there had me frozen in fear. Seeing Di Pietro lying on the ground, dying, had me speechless. I'd seen death many times in the three years I've ran this place but facing the death of this man felt different. The scene had left me frozen, and it was only when Noè coaxed me back into the club that the anger I usually felt finally hit me. I'd been paralyzed, and he bore witness to my show of weakness. It infuriated me.

"Boss, you want me to take you home?" Luca offers instead of me walking into this house. Four of my other boys stood around the house, standing vigil for Di Pietro. Others would come later, as the clubs closed and the Irish were hunted down.

"No," I answer, starting my walk to the front door. I knock, and Irene opens the door for me. Inside, the sobbing of her mother could be heard. The same woman who had toasted me at *Petit Coeur*. The same woman who opened her home and gave me a place at her table when I lost my parents and brother. That woman now regretting ever letting her husband or daughter get involved in my business.

Titone and Renzi both stood inside, their wives sitting with Mrs. Di Pietro to comfort her. Doriano stood with the two men, as his son-in-law and none of his other children being involved in the business yet, Doriano now stood in for Di Pietro. If the man died tonight, then his son-in-law would be the one to take over his side of the business.

Irene stands beside me, and I wonder where Noè is, surely, he came to the home with them. He wouldn't leave Irene in this position, Doriano in this position. Technically, while here, he is the head of the Chicago Italian Mafia. Leaving an injured man would be entirely uncalled for in this situation.

"Boss," both Titone and Renzi greet me, their

wives all turning their heads up. Mrs. Di Pietro meets my gaze, tears staining her face. I go over to her first, ignoring the men in the room. I kneel in front of the older woman who fed me many nights when I sat in her living room working with her husband and daughter.

"Is he still alive?" She nods at me, and I sigh in relief. I hear footsteps coming down the stairs. It is Noè, I can feel it. I don't turn though; I focus on the women grieving in front of me. "He's a good man, a strong man. He'll be alright."

"What about the bastard that shot him?" Doriano asks from behind the couch.

"He's dead," Noè replies from the doorway. "It the accomplices that got away."

"Two died on the scene," I explain to Mrs. Di Pietro what I assume she didn't know. I decided not to mention the warehouse. A glance at Renzi tells me he knows about the attack. As my manager of shipments and distribution, the warehouses are under his control. He would know that Cristiano stole guns from me tonight, killing two of our workers and leaving behind four bodies of his own. I turn back to the crying woman and make her a promise, "The other two will die as well, by my hand."

"The enforcers have it?" Titone asks me. He knows the answer, the actions of the Irish tonight will be answered with death.

"They do," I assure them all. "Blood for blood."

"Blood for blood," Titone replies, then Renzi and Doriano echo.

I stand then, turning to look at Noè. A light bruise is forming under an eye, his chin swollen slightly, and a lip busted with a fresh wound. He wasn't shot though, and he stood tall as if nothing in his stomach hurt. His pride would be wounded but he is alive, and he is okay.

"How is he?" I ask the man standing in the doorway. Renzi clearly didn't like his presence, judging by the scowl he used to look at Noè. Titone masked his disapproval better, merely crossing his arms and staring at the Bendoni the way he would one of the boys that had been asked a question. A look that demanded he answer me.

Noè turns form me to Mrs. Di Pietro, "He's awake and asking for you." The older woman sighs, standing to rush up the stair to his bedside. I give Irene a small smile and nod, silently telling her to follow. She takes Doriano's hand, following her mother up the stairs.

I face Renzi fully, "You know about the warehouse?"

"I heard."

"What about the warehouse?" Noè took another step into the room, moving closer to me. Titone and Renzi moved as well, the larger Titone stepping between him and me. They were always protective of me, Titone moreso than Renzi, and after Cristiano's threats and tonight's events, my advisors are even more cautious.

"He is not a threat," I remind them. He is my boss, and he has a right to know how I've failed again tonight. The Irish attacked my men outside my club while Cristiano stole guns from under my nose. My cousin is waging war on me, and I've given him all the ammo he needs to make his power legit. I cannot rule. Tonight made it clear.

Noè's father would come here and give it to him at Cristiano's first request. Even though it had been him that stole from me, robbery was a cardinal sin in our world, and he'd walked away with my guns alive.

"Cristiano broke into one of the warehouses and stole guns. We believe he fled the cities, which means he's probably on his way to New York to plead with your father once more to take this from me forcefully and after tonight, he should."

"Boss," Titone starts but I held up my hand to stop him.

"We had a great three years together boys, but I have a choice to make. Give Di Pietro my love." With that I leave, knowing that my next move has to be calculated and correct. I made my way back home on foot with Luca close behind me. I enjoy the night air as the wind off the lake blows my curls off my neck. My thoughts entirely on my choice.

Cristiano will petition, and Bendoni will give him what he wants unless I can place a male on the throne myself. Chicago has done fine with a solo queen, but to remain on my throne I'll need a consort. Di Pietro always made me a list, and now I'd call on them to come courting. Someone to protect me when Cristiano came to take it all from me the way he believes I took it all from him.

My home is dark and silent when I arrive. Nonno and Beth are already asleep and safe in their rooms. I take a seat in my office, pulling out the last list Di Pietro, seeing his name at the top. His name is always at the top of my lists, like a silent plea for me to choose him. Three years of lists, and apparently three years of letters to Noè about my activities. I had been so mad about those letters, but I also understood how hesitant the Bendonis must be about my leadership. A woman leading the mafia, four years ago I would have laughed at the idea. No doubt so would my father and brother. Yet they left it to me, probably hoping I'd marry immediately and give Chicago a king instead of the queen they have now.

The door opened, and I didn't have to look to find out who it was. My back tingled and my heart jumped when he comes into the room. I know what decision to make, but to admit it makes me want to cry. I hadn't wanted this when my father and brother died, I hadn't wanted to rule. Now, the thought of even giving up a fraction of my freedom made me cringe. Yet, letting Cristiano take it from me is out of the question. He cannot have my throne, which means I have to share it.

"Miss Sanna?"

CHAPTER 17

Noè Bendoni

I found her in her office, staring over a piece of paper. Her list. The one Di Pietro had made for her regularly over the past three years to encourage her to marry someone. She had never even considered courting, from what I gathered. Always thanking him for the lists and tucking them away, disregarded.

Now she had to consider them, knowing that her failures would outshine her victories in my father's eyes after police went into her club after a shooting right outside. Now after, on the same night, Cristiano stole from her. Even if it was her cousin that conspired in the crimes and worked with the Irish, he would see the ease with which they were committed as a sign of her weakness. My thoughts on the matter would not be considered, not again. She would need to protect herself, and the best way to do that now is through nuptials.

My curiosity strikes me, wanting to know

which names she's considering to court. I knew my name is among them, but so are many viable suitors. Many mafia men who would drop everything at a chance to rule this city. Chicago is a stronghold -- and it has only gotten richer since Addy took over. Any mafia man, young or old, would give anything for even the small chance to rule it.

I stop halfway through the doorway to greet her, "Miss Sanna." Her chuckle at my call is uncomfortably sinister. Not like the woman I've known for the past week, and definitely not like the woman I drank and danced with tonight. It is cruel in some ways, and sad in others. It chills me deep into my bones.

"It is 'Miss Sanna' again? Now that you know the choice I face you address me as lady and not a friend." Her words bit at me, and I immediately regret my choice of greeting. It was too cold for us. For the "us" we've become.

"Addy," I correct, but it is only her name I get out.

"Make your choice, Bendoni." My name sounds like a curse on her lips, and I cringe.

"Adelaide Sanna," I say this time and she turns to face me; her eyebrows rise in a slight challenge. In her eyes, I see all her emotions, as clear as the sky. They've widened like a dear cornered by wolves. "It shouldn't be just anyone. I can help you choose him. I know most of the men on that list and will help you find one you can trust."

She stands, leaving the list on her desk, "You are on the list."

I smile and tease her, "Is that a proposal?"

"Do you want it to be?" Her voice flat, not joking.

I stop then and we both just stare at one another. I contemplated her question, wondering if she's made her own decision on the matter. Was I her choice? Being the only man on that list she knew, it made sense. Her decision to marry is now forced, something she never wanted to happen. Something I never wanted to happen to her. Any choice she makes now, I would honor it.

Even if that choice wasn't me, which I know from my chest tightening, I didn't want. I want her to choose me now, make me her *re*.

Taking a deep breath, I reply, "Do you?"

"Men have always tried to make choices for me. You haven't tried to do it once this week. That is something even Di Pietro isn't innocent of. Why?"

"I'm different," I assure her, reaching for her face. "I want you to choose."

I want you to choose me.

"And you'll respect my choice?" Addy leans into my touch, comforting herself in my warmth.

"Yes," I promise her. "Choose your *re, mia regina*. Choose wisely but the choice is yours."

She takes another step into me, pressing our chests together. Her hands rest on my chest, out breath mingling as she looks from her hands to my eyes. Her tongue darts out to wet her lips as she stares at me. Determination burns in those eyes, drawing me in to her. The urge to kiss her tightens my chest and makes it harder and harder to breathe. I can't kiss her though, not until she's made her choice.

"You know already..." she breathes out, her eyes darting to my lips.

"You have to say it. Make it real, Adelaide."

"I choose you, Noè Bendoni." I lean down, brushing my lips against her then. A soft gasp escapes her before I actually capture her lips in a hard kiss. We mold together, sharing our embrace. I pull back, letting it end sooner than I'd like, but it needs to end. She chooses me, but as the man, I'm the one who has to ask.

"I have no ring for you now," I breathe out, my forehead touching hers. My lower lip burns from the cut it bore from my earlier fight, but I ignore it. I'm determined to kiss her again tonight. "I will get you one though, make it all proper for you."

"I don't need it all proper."

I chuckle, cupping her face with both my hands, "Yet you shall have it, because you are worth it. Now be quiet so I can ask the damn question." She giggles as I kiss the very tip of her nose. "Adelaide Sanna, *mia regina,* will you marry me?"

"Is that your final proposal?"

"Absolutely."

"Yes." I kiss her again and she stumbles back from the force her legs pressed against her desk as we kiss. My hands move to her back, holding her closer to me as our lips dance. Her arms wrap around my neck, her finger gripping my blonde hair. I kiss her cheek and chin before resting my head on her shoulder. Her chest rises and falls quickly, her own lips falling on my ear to leave a kiss there.

"Noè," she whispers right over my ear, brushing my skin with her lips when she spoke. Desire for more of this woman courses though me and my hands itch to touch every inch of Addy.

"Yes?" I reply, turning my head to face her neck, and placing another kiss on her skin. Damn it, she tastes so good. Her skin is so soft and unmarred. I place one more kiss on her neck and she draws in a quick breath. Only one more, I only allow myself one more.

If I don't stop now, then I'll do something ungentlemanly.

"Sunday."

"As in basically tomorrow Sunday?"

"Yes."

"That's not a lot of time," I remind her, stealing another kiss onto her neck. She shutters and her fingers dig into my scalp.

"I don't want anything fancy, I just want it done."

"Very romantic," I laugh, then move so I can

face her. I need some distance between me and her delicate skin.

"We don't have a lot of time," she reminds me with a silent plea in her eyes. "Once Cristiano is back--"

"He's dead," I growl, squeezing her hips. "For stealing from you, for threatening you, he is dead."

"But he will bring your father, and when he comes it has to be done."

I give her a nod, agreeing. It had to be done before Cristiano comes back with my father. He won't accept anything but a legal and godly wedding. And while it was short notice, the sooner I married this woman the happier I would be in my life. Having *mia regina* at my side forever would improve my outlook on life. Facing her smug cousin with rings on our fingers would definably improve my mood.

"If we're getting married this weekend you should definitely go get some sleep," I tell her, giving her a peck on her lips. I really can't stop myself.

After being obsessed with her for three years, kissing her is like a drug. One I will happily form an addiction too and never give up. One I never want to be sober of. She's an obsession that will last a lifetime.

She nods, and we leave her office to go upstairs, I walk her to her room, the one across from mine. She opens the door, turning to me before entering. "You killed those men in the alley."

Addy wasn't questioning me, more of a verification of the events. She touches the cut on my lip. It burns under her gentle fingers, but I try not to show the pain. I don't want her to stop touching me. Ever. "I did. I killed the man that shot Di Pietro and the one that attacked me."

"And the other two?"

"Once I killed the shooter, Doriano's attacker ran, and the other was quick to follow. I couldn't chase them because you came out," I explain. "I saw you and knew I couldn't leave you there."

"Thank you."

"There is no need for that. Go to sleep now."

"Stay...?"

As much as her offer enticed me, to stay would be frowned upon. We might be engaged now, and married in less than 48 hours, but I couldn't stay. All those Sunday school lessons my mother forced me into came rushing back and I couldn't stay. Mother would kill me if I stay.

"Sunday night," I promise her, kissing her forehead. "Sunday night I will stay."

She nods, "Goodnight, Noè."

"Goodnight, Addy."

CHAPTER 18

Adelaide Sanna

O n Saturday we went to the church, Father David was free after mass, meaning we could get married the day we'd chosen last night. After that, we both went to the Di Pietro house with a casserole for the family. All their children were there. One of the older boys took the dish while Irene took me upstairs to the injured man. He lay flat in bed, his wife steadfast by his side. He'd always called her the perfect wife, the perfect mafia wife, especially. When I married, I always told myself I'd be like her. If it was Noè that had been shot, no doubt I would not leave his bedside.

"Can I have a moment alone with him?" I ask and Mrs. Di Pietro nods before kissing his cheek and leaving. I take her place at his side in the chair. "You old idiot."

He chuckled before coughing, "How am I the one shot and the one blamed?"

"You should have shot first," I answer with a

small smile. "Cristiano will pay. Blood for blood."

"You're not just here to promise revenge. If I didn't think you'd get revenge for this, I would have never helped you take over three years ago."

"I had to make a tough decision, a fast one. Cristiano had fled the city, and we think he went to Bendoni to beg again."

"Noè won't let him--"

"Noè wouldn't have had a say this time," I tell him. "But I'm giving him that power to protect me."

Di Pietro's eyes go wide, and he coughs again. I pass him a glass of water and help him drink. "When?"

"Tomorrow," I tell him with a small smile. "I'll be a married women and Cristiano can't stop it. Bendoni won't dethrone his son."

"Smart girl, I always hoped you'd pick him."

"Why him?"

"He's ruthless, but protective and loyal. Every time your father and I would go to New York, he was always generous with us. Your father picked him, actually, not me."

"What?"

"He was waiting until you were twenty before making the introduction. He had it all arranged, which is why I wasn't surprised when Noè started asking about you after their death. He never pushed for the introduction, even though it had been promised to him, he just wanted to hear about all your accomplishments. That was really what those letters were about."

"I see," is all I respond. I didn't know my father well; I was a young child when I went to live with Auntie Ellen and Uncle David. Angelo was almost ten years older than me. We lived entirely different lives, and I had only visited Chicago on a rare occasion. To know he had made plans for me, without even really knowing me, boiled my blood slightly. To know that man he planned for me was Noè, it made me less angry. Because I too had chosen this man for myself.

A knock came, and Noè enters with one of my enforcers. "Sorry to interrupt, boss."

"What is it?"

"The man who shot Di Pietro, we got his brother. He's young so he's talking."

I stand, glancing back at the bed-ridden man. He gave a nod, "Blood for blood."

I leave with the enforcer and Noè and we go to one of the older warehouses. The roof leaked here, so no merchandise was kept on the lot. It was mostly used for prisoners and executions. Three enforcers circled the boy, barely eighteen by my guess. No hair on his face and the short curly brown hair atop his head reminded me of one of Di Pietro's sons.

He gasps as I walked into the room, stiffened and shifting his eyes between me and Noè. Probably wondering which of us would kill him. I had a reputation in this city, but Noè exerted a deadly aurora as we walked into the room.

"I asked for the two living ones," I remind the enforcers. "Where are the two that attacked them that escaped?"

"We are still looking," August says to me, a newer enforcer of mine that rose to his position by being a club bodyguard.

"What about those that stole from me?"

"We're tracking them down, following leads as we speak, boss," another enforcer, Martin, assures me.

"Find them." August and another left, Martin and two more staying as my shields for when I decided what to do with this boy. I turn to him then, fear melting off of him. "Your name?"

"*Banríon fraochún*," he spits out. My three enforcers stiffened, circling the boy ready to kill him.

"What did he say?" Noè asks me.

"He said 'whore queen,'" I tell him. "It is their fun nickname for me."

Noè then stocks up to the boy, grabbing his neck in one hand. A scared choking sound croaks out of his mouth. Color drains from his face as Noè growls out, "That is my wife, *stronzo irlandese*. You want to try again?" The boy nods before taking a large gasp of air as Noè lets him go. "Apologize."

"I am sorry, Ma'am," he coughs out. "I am Richard."

"Richard," I draw out. "Your brother attacked my men outside my club. I don't know how you inbreds do it, but in the mafia, we rule blood for blood."

"My brothers are dead. You have your blood."

"Two helped them and lived," I explain. "I want their names."

"No."

"Tell her," Noè orders. The boy defied the order, keeping his mouth shut.

"How many brothers do you have?" I ask next, seeing panic start to take his features. He doesn't answer. "Martin?"

"They breed like rabbits, I'm not sure how many there are."

"At least four, right?" I turn back to the boy. "Two died, two escaped."

"Blood for blood," the boy squeaks.

Noè looks at me, waiting for my next move. "Find his brothers," I direct to Martin. "And feed the boy."

I leave and my fiancé follows me. He drives me back to my house. The midafternoon sun glimmers off the windows of the car. The drive is short, and neither of us speak. It is comfortable though, a silence that lets me think on the boy whose brothers attacked Noè, Doriano, and Di Pietro. He seems too young to be in this mess. I'd killed men before, both by my hand and ordering their deaths. Men, not boys.

Once we get to the house, Nonno sat outside on the porch with Beth. His eyes closed and tilted back to feel the warmth on his face. I sit beside him, taking his hand and kissing his cheek.

"Adelaide," he calls to me. "Where is momma?"

"No, Nonno. It's your granddaughter, not your sister." I've had to remind him more and more often that I am not my namesake.

"Where is Luciano?"

"He's dead, Nonno."

"Oh... did you tell Ivan not to marry that *troia*?"

"You mean Aunt Emma?"

"Don't say her name, Luciano."

"No, Nonno, I'm Adelaide." I look at Beth and then to Noè. Beth gave me a small sympathetic smile, while Noè simply rested his hand on my shoulder.

"I told him that boy wasn't ours. He... he was always blind to a good smile."

"Nonno, I am very confused."

"Don't marry her, Ivan!" Nonno grabs my arm, gripping my wrist tight. I wince under his hold and Noè goes to remove him. I stop him, grabbing his hand with my free one.

"Why not?"

"That boy isn't ours. He isn't ours."

"Which boy?"

"You can pretend, Ivan, but I know. You may give him my name, but he will never belong to this family."

"Who?"

"Emma's boy."

"Cristiano?" I question next, but Nonno goes silent and releases my arm. His face relaxing from the anger it had just displayed. "Nonno, is the boy Cristiano?" He closed his eyes, turning back up to the sun. I knew the look well; he wouldn't speak anymore. His mind had gone blank again.

"Are you okay?" Noè asks quietly from behind me. I stand from my seat and go inside my family home with my fiancé right behind me. My father's old office waited for me, little had been changed in the house in three years. His office, now mine, hadn't been changed at all. It felt wrong to redecorate any of it. "Addy, wait."

I start to search his records; he had all our paperwork kept in one of the lower cabinets. I found it all shortly after I took over: birth, marriage, and death certificates all kept neatly together. Nonno's and Nonna's immigration paperwork. My father and three uncles' birth certificates and their marriage licenses. It is there I find Ivan's marriage to Emma, and Cristiano's birth certificate. A four-month difference.

"Emma was pregnant before they got married," I state, putting out all the paperwork on the desk.

"You think he isn't your uncle's son?" Noè asks from the doorway.

"Nonno obviously does," I look up to my fiancé and give him a small smile. "Cristiano isn't a Sanna."

"Maybe not by blood, but there is no way to prove it," he reminds me, stalking over to stand beside me. His hand falls lazily on my waist.

"Legally, your uncle claimed him as a Sanna by marrying Emma and giving him the name. It may help your case in keeping Chicago, but it does not save you."

"No, I know," I turn to look up at him, snaking my arms around his neck. "I still plan on marrying you, if that's what you mean."

Noè kisses my forehead, "Good."

"It just means we have to fight harder. He can't have my family's legacy."

"He won't have it," Noè promises me. "I will protect you."

"I know you will."

CHAPTER 20

Noè Bendoni

Sunday morning, we go to mass. After mass, the congregation is invited to stay and witness our wedding. Irene stands with Addy, and as much as I wish my brother was here, he isn't, so Doriano stands with me. Beth brought Addy's nonno and Mary the housekeeper came as well. Half of her whole organization came to church on Sunday to attend the wedding.

Addy wears a long, straight frame wedding dress. Her skirt was adorned with lace and her white gloves were silk and soft in my own hands. Father David performs the ceremony, and we say our vows. We exchange rings, rings from her Nonno and Nonna's wedding. Both rings were simple gold bands, and we share a giddy smile as we place the rings on each other's fingers. Finally, I kiss her, solidifying her as mine. It is a short, simple kiss, but at the end as I am about to pull away, she nibbles on my lower lip.

I give her a dark glance as she giggles at

me. We return to her family home where we eat and drink all afternoon. We share many kisses and glances as we celebrate with those that joined us from her organization. They would come and go, greeting me with hesitant respect. By all Italian mafia traditions and American inheritance law, I am the boss here now. Yet, as I expected, they all still look to her for answers on how it will work now.

She is the queen of Chicago; I'm simply her consort. I was always born to be a second. My father planned on it being to my brother, but I chose her. I will follow her and support her. I will protect her and be a good second the way my father always wanted. Her protector.

An assurance that it will never be taken from her. I'm her security that will protect her from all those that wish to harm her. Cristiano, specifically, but if my father decides to join that list then so be it.

"Congratulations, Mr. Bendoni," Irene says to me, offering her hand. I take it and shake. She is alone, her husband sitting with her mother in the dining room.

"Addy sees you as a sister," I state, not needing conformation but accepting her nod. "You are family, call me Noè."

"We are family, Addy and I, meaning if you hurt her in any way, there will be hell."

"I'm sure that goes for you and the rest of the men that follow her."

"You should fear me more," Irene says with a smile and a pat to my arm.

Around four o'clock, the crowd begins to disperse. Addy and I climb into one of her cars and took a short drive to an apartment I signed for yesterday. Knowing we would want some seclusion in the evenings from her nonno and Beth. The simple one-bedroom apartment was sparsely decorated, but cozy in a way. I carried my bride inside, both of us falling onto the small sofa in the parlor.

Addy settles into my lap, kissing my cheek. Her head lolled onto my shoulder as we relaxed from the long day. My body buzzes with excitement and alcohol from our party. Her arms wrap around my neck, and we share a peck. Addy hums as she presses her lips to my neck. Electricity bolts though me, tightening my stomach and exciting my cock.

"Can I ask you a question?" she mutters against my skin.

"Anything, *mia regina*."

"How many other women have you been with?"

I turn to her, shocked at the question. "A few."

"How many?"

I give her a boyish grin, "Not many, but a few. Maybe three."

"Your smile at this annoys me, it is no joke."

"I know," I place a kiss on her nose. "I'm no

virgin, but I'm no whore either. None since I met you."

"I am a virgin."

"That is good," I nibble on her ear. "I had hoped you were." She breathes out a sigh as I continue to kiss and bite on her ear lobe.

"I did kiss a boy once, when I lived downstate."

"Addy," I blew on her neck, causing her to shiver. "We are going to have problems if you're thinking about some hick boy when I'm kissing you."

"I'm just nervous," she admits. "Irene told me it took time before she enjoyed being with Doriano."

"I'm not Doriano," I remind her sharply. She starts to shift, and I move with her. Her legs separate to straddle me so we can be face-to-face. Her breathe fans across my face, and I sign in content just to hold her. My wife. My queen. "I will make sure you enjoy it."

"How?" I give her a devilish look, before bunching up her skirt around her hips. I touch her soft skin there, sliding my fingers along the band on her kickers. Then, I move them up her sides, brushing my thumbs against her silk brassiere. She gasps.

"Take off your dress," I order her. Addy quickly stands and removes the garment along with her pretty shoes, leaving her probably as bare as she's ever been in front of a man. I hold out my hand to her, drawing her back to me.

We kiss once more, her teeth nibbling on my lower lip the way she had in the church. I lick her lips, pushing my tongue past them and into her mouth. She moans then, grinding herself against me. I undo her brassiere, freeing her of it. My thumb runs over her peaks again and she shivers and moans.

"You're beautiful, *mia regina*," I whisper. Her fingers fumble with the buttons of my shirt, pushing my jacket off my shoulder. I help her remove my jacket as she continues working on the buttons of my shirt.

As I strip down, Addy places her lips on my neck, nibbling on my skin. I reach between us, sliding my hands up her knickers and massaging her thighs. I grab her firmly before standing from the sofa. She yelps, holding onto me as I reconnect our lips. Intertwined, we go to the bedroom. I toss her onto the bed, tugging on the last of her undergarments. Her knickers fly across the room, and she turns red.

The bed dips as I climb over her, kissing up her body. My lips wrap around one of her nipples, sucking. She gasps, moaning while fingers dig into my hair. Equal attention is given to the other one before kissing her neck and cheek. She tastes like home, like this is exactly where I am supposed to be tonight. Not New York. Not *Italia*. Here. With her.

When I touch the nub between her legs, she

whimpers. "You're wet," I chuckle, playing with her folds and sliding my fingers up to put pressure on the small bundle at the top of her core, and she squirms.

"Is that..." she gasps. "Good?"

"Very good," I grumble as I kiss her again, our tongues dancing together. Her hips buck upward when I push one finger inside her. My wife wiggles and squirms and I curl my finger.

"Noè," she calls out, digging her nails into my shoulder.

"Are you enjoying yourself?" I coo into her ear.

"Yes," she hisses, pressing her hips into me once more.

"Do you want more?"

"Yes," she responds, and I chuckle. "I want you."

Addy groans when I remove my finger from her to remove my pants. I undo my belt and buttons before I can slide them off. Addy watches me undress with blatant curiosity. When at last all of me was visible to my wife, her eyes widened.

"No..."

"You'll be okay, darling," I promise her. "It won't feel good at first, but I promise it will."

"I trust you," she nods. I give her a smile, kissing her as I position myself to enter. She tenses under me, and I stop.

"*Mia regina*," I coo to her. Our eyes meet and I caress her cheek. "Relax, darling."

"You said it will hurt," she complains.

I push my finger back inside her, my thumb rubbing her nub. Addy moans. "Does this hurt?"

"No. I like that."

"Good," I kiss her neck. "And you'll like the rest too." I remove my finger, repositioning myself. She looks down, watching my member. "Eyes here, pretty girl."

She uses her eyes to bore into my soul, my tip presses into her and she winces. Her eyes close tight and I brush my thumb over her cheek. Addy opens her eyes again and I reward her with a kiss. As our lips meet, I thrust into her. I groan, feeling her around me. Slowly, I pull out and thrust back in. She whimpers, holding me close to her as I slowly thrust in and out. My stomach tightens with my steady pace.

Addy moans and wraps her legs around me as our hips meet over and over. I grab her soft hips, shifting to go deeper inside her. My body tingles and my legs ache from the work. My wife whines and moans beneath me. I've been with other women, but nothing compared to driving into my wife. The air between us grows hot and I know I'm getting close. Using my fingers on her and kissing her to make sure she enjoys this as much as I do, she cries out my name.

"I-- I--," she pants out, gripping my shoulders and squeezing my hips with her legs. She tightens around my member, and I know she's close. "Noè."

"I know, *reginetta*," I purr in her ear, placing a kiss below it. My release comes quickly, and I groan, trusting through the heights of my pleasure. Addy joins me at the peak, her hips meeting mine in every movement. As our heartrates slow again, I pull all the way out to lay next to Addy. Using my arm as a pillow, my queen curls next to me.

"That was," she sighs. "Amazing."

I chuckle at her, then sit up and pull her into my lap. I move us to the top of the bed, pulling on the sheets and quilt to put us underneath. "You are amazing, wife."

"I'm happy I picked you."

"I'm happy too," I admit. We curl together; our naked bodies molded perfectly to one another. "I'm glad you enjoyed it."

"Did you enjoy it?" she pops up beside me, leaning over me. Hair fans around her head, showering me with the scent of flowers.

I lean forward to kiss her nose, "More than anything."

"More than the other girls?"

"Definitely more than the others."

Addy falls back to my side, smiling. "Good."

CHAPTER 21

Adelaide Bendoni

Light from the single bedroom window wakes me up. My body stretches, stiff from the way I had curled into my husband last night. My insides are sore, and when I close my eyes, I can still see Noè over me, still feel him inside me. Beside me, his blonde hair is covering his eyes. The messy yet peaceful look so different from what I've come to expect of him. I brush away his hair, cupping his cheek. The black eyes from Friday night still decorates his face and the cut on his lip is still fresh and red.

As I get up, I wince from the soreness between my legs. The slight discomfort makes me smile though, remembering how gentle he has been with me and the pleasure he made me feel. He had all our essentials delivered to the apartment yesterday, and in the wardrobe, I find a robe to cover my bare body. I get ready for the day as quietly as possible to not wake up Noè.

In the kitchen, I find some breakfast and

coffee. A sound from the hallways calls my attention before a knock at the door. Irene stands on the other side with Felix, I double check that the bedroom door is closed before letting them inside.

"The marriage license was filed this morning, and the lawyer has been made aware of the union," Irene begins, handing me copies of all the paperwork. "He wants to meet with both of you and your grandfather to adjust his will to include Mr. Bendoni."

"Nonno isn't in his right mind to do that. We will leave the will as is and when he passes Noè will just take over my share."

"Alright," Irene gives me a small smile. I can see the question rolling around in her brain, but I also know she won't ask about my wedding night in front of Felix.

"We found the two men from the club, they are at the same warehouse as the boy," Felix tells me, and I nod in understanding. They will pay for the pain they have inflicted on my family. No doubt the enforcers didn't bring them in painlessly. Even if they didn't resist, I expected these too Irishmen to have bruises and broken bones.

"Any news on Cristiano?"

"None yet, but we are monitoring train stations and those on our payroll in the police force know if he is seen he should be brought to us," Felix adds.

The door to the bedroom opens then, Noè

stands there, thankfully in a robe. He gives me a warm smile before turning to Felix and Irene. "I didn't realize we had guests."

"Wait outside and we will go to the warehouse," I order them both, walking them to the door.

"Back to business already?" Noè asks as he pours himself a cup of coffee. "I didn't realize that our honeymoon would only last one night."

I debate telling him the news on the Irish attackers. Last week I wouldn't have told him, simply executed them and had it over with. He's the head of the Chicago operations now, though, and it is his right to know. Yet, a small part of me is afraid to say anything. He is now the boss here and I am just his wife. It is well within his power to take full control and not let me handle any of it again. I had always feared that over the years, having it all taken away from me by either Cristiano or my husband. I hadn't wanted to answer to anyone in that way, and now I was in that position.

He held power over me. More than before. Before, he was my boss. A Bendoni.

Now, he is my husband.

And now is the time to find out if I was right about him. If I was right to trust him. So, I tell him, because I have too, "They found the two Irishmen that attacked on Friday."

His expression turns cold, "Good, I'll get dressed and we can go."

"We?"

"Yes," he furrows his eyebrows. "You and me. We. Us."

"I will still... be in charge?"

"I won't lord over you, Addy." He holds out his hand to me, beckoning me to him. I take his hand, allowing him to pull me close. I rest my hands on his chest, as his encircle my waist and we hold each other close. "This is your city, *reginetta*. You make the decisions here and I will support you in them. I won't ever force you to give up running this city. I will only ask one thing." I give him a small nod to continue. "When we have children, you take a step back when they are young. Not complete give it all up but let me do more while they are babes."

A smile spreads across my face, "I won't take them to executions if that's what you mean."

"That," he chuckles with me. "And I want to make sure you're not stressed when we have children. I don't want you to overwork yourself."

"I understand," I push up onto my toes to kiss him. "When that time comes, I will step back but I never want to leave completely."

"I will never ask that of you," Noè assures me. "Let us get dressed and we will go to the warehouse."

The warehouse was cold, despite the warm sun

outside. Richard, the young boy, sat between his two brothers. The older boys were bloody and bruised, meanwhile Richard wasn't touched. My men knew the boy hadn't done anything wrong, and with no Italians dying in the attack, he wouldn't pay for his brothers' crimes. Noè walked just behind me as we entered the main room of the warehouse. Five other enforcers waited for us, with Felix leading us into the room. Irene never comes with for these things, Di Pietro and Doriano forbidding her from seeing death.

"Ma'am, please," Richard pleads. "They're my brothers."

"Di Pietro is like my father, and they had no problem shooting him. Doriano is like my brother, and they had no problem beating him." The men squirm as I explain the circumstances to their brother. I point to the one who looks older, he had golden hair and a growing pale beard. "You. Tell me why."

"He said if we helped him then we'd be helping dismantle the Italians."

"Who?"

"He said if we snuck in the back of the club we'd have a clear shot at you."

"I was your target?" The club opening was very public, very publicized. The whole of Chicago and many of the surrounding towns knew it would open that night; we wanted the place packed for maximum profit. Usually on a Friday night, I would bounce from club to club, and no one knew where exactly I was going to be except my men. That night, the whole city knew exactly where I would be, and that I would be vulnerable from the celebration.

"Said we needed to kill you and not hurt the blonde at your side," the man gestured to Noè and fresh blood dripped from his nose at the movement. "Said we couldn't kill him. When we saw the three out back, we thought if we took them out, we'd be clear to get you. Had no idea he was the one we weren't supposed to hurt."

"Who hired you?" I ask next. My suspicions were obvious to all of mine in the room, but we needed prove Cristiano tried to have me killed. The man shut his swollen lips tight though, so I turned to the other who has yet to speak. He shared the color of hair as his brother, but his baby-face had no hair. "You tell me."

"One of you should answer her," Noè growls from behind me.

"He came to Pa first," Richard blurts out. His older brother with the beard hushed him and red spittle went flying through the air.

"Keep going."

"Pa said he was one of us, blood. We could trust him."

"His name?"

"Cristiano."

"Blood how?"

"Our Pa is his Pa."

"Who is your 'pa'?"

"Richie, shut up," his bearded brother growls. "You don't owe this bitch an explanation. She's gonna kill us."

Noè shifts from behind me to the man, his fists collide with his already hurt face. Blood falls from his lips as my husband grabs his throat, choking the man the way he had with Richard when he has insulted me. "Watch your mouth in front of the lady, I can make your death a lot worse than it needs to be if you spew that filth about my wife."

"Please let him go," Richard begs, but Noè doesn't relent. Lips turn blue and his face turns red before he is allowed air again. Noè steps back to my side, placing his hand on my waist. The man coughs and chokes as he gasps in air. I don't react to the sight and neither do any of my men.

"Cristiano is their brother, he is no Sanna. He isn't even Italian, he's Irish," I state aloud, for all my enforcers to hear. Noè's hand squeezes my side, and he kisses the side of my head. My husband still has murder in his eyes, staring down the man that had called me a 'bitch.' I copy him, wrapping my arm around him and squeezing him back. My touch draws his gaze down to me, the murder dissipates, and his features soften. "Do you want to kill them?"

His gaze shifts over my face, searching for something I'm not sure. "Yes."

I nod, turning to Felix who pulls out his gun for Noè. "Keep Richard alive."

"I want a knife," Noè tells Felix instead. He goes to a cabinet in the corner of the room, unlocking it and opening it to displace a wide array of different knives. I walk Noè over to the cabinet, and stare at one blade I have used a thousand times over the past three years. I take it for him. A small blade about three inches in length with a nice wooden handle.

"This is my favorite," I tell him, flipping it to pass it to him handle first. He smiles at me, a week smile, but one that is truly all Noè. A small smile just for me. Then it went away, and he turned from me and back to them men who attacked them. He stalks towards them, going first to the man who cooperated. I watch from the side, waiting to see what the man I'd heard was so ruthless can truly do.

He slit his throat, letting blood spatter across the room. It stained Noè's chest, and droplets land across the floor. Not the first time this floor has been stained red. Richard whimpers and his eyes water as he watched his brother choke on his own blood. When his head lolls to the side, Noè moves on to the other.

He passes Richard, doing as I instructed and letting the boy live, to the brother who called me a "bitch." My husband's dark eyes bore down at the man, and he squirms. He knows now that he messed up, that he will die slower and more painfully than his brother.

Noè starts by cutting off the rest of his

shirt, leaving his hairy chest exposed. He starts to carve. Flesh torn and shredded under the blade I gave him. Noè's warmth, his humor, his *remorse* is gone in those minutes, replaced by a man I didn't know. Yet, one I had no fear of seeing. He carves lines and lines over the chest, opening up the flesh to muscle, then deeper. His hands stain red. The Irishman screamed, he screamed and begged for mercy. He prayed to God to make it end, but not even God himself could stop what was happening. No one would save this man from *re mio*'s blade.

I hear it when the blade hits bone, Noè filets the skin open between his ribs, but the movements aren't exactly presence as he squirms and screams and tries to get away from the torment. He carves open his belly, letting the knife sink in as deep as it will go, into his vital organs no doubt.

When Noè is satisfied with the man's chest, he steps back and admires his work for a second. Then, just for good measure, as the man pants to try and catch his breath, Noè grabs his jaw, forces his mouth open, and removes his tongue. It happens so quickly that the man doesn't even know it is happening until the blood is running down his throat and into his lungs. It is a painful death to watch, but I watch the whole ordeal.

Noè returns the knife to the cabinet and washes his hands and face in a sink. He cleans off his skin until the only blood left on his is on the white of his shirt. One of the enforcers brings him a fresh one from another room and he quickly changes.

He looks over one more time at his kill, then to me. "Let's go," I call to Noè.

Outside the warehouse, when we are alone, Noè grabs my wrists, pulling me back to him. I'm spun into his arm and our lips meet. He kisses me harshly, nibbling on my lip and gripping my waist to hold me close.

"What was that for?" I ask when he pulls away.

"Reminding myself that Cristiano didn't kill you."

"No," I run my thumb over his split lip and up to his black eye. "But he got you good."

This will heal." He kisses me again. "If those *figlio di puttana* had gotten to you that night, I don't know what I'd do."

"You wouldn't be married," I remind him.

"That's right, I'm married now," he jokes, pulling me closer to his chest. "So, Mrs. Bendoni, what do you say we go home?"

"Why would we go home?" I tease him.

"Because I want some quality time with my wife," he growls in my ear. Noè pulls me back to the car, his arm wrapped around me as we drive back to our small apartment. His fingers burn to my side as the late spring wind blows through the car windows. His thumb runs up and down my hip, reminding me of the things he did to me last night with that thumb. I lean into his side, burying my face into his shoulder. Tilting my head, I stretch up and kiss his neck. He responds with a squeeze on my hip. Another kiss, another squeeze.

I remember how he licked and nibbled me, how it had made my stomach tighten and my core weep. The next kiss I give, I nibble on his skin. Taking the flesh between my teeth and tugging gently, licking over the spot when I finish. Noè groans this time.

"Stop it or I will crash this car," he orders. I slide my hand over his stomach, placing it at the top of his thigh. Heat radiates off my husband as he turns down our street; the anticipation for what is to come boils inside me.

Kisses are traced up his neck before I latch onto his ear lobe, sucking hard on his flesh. The car stops quickly, and I am jerked forward. Noè grabs me, securing me to the seat with his arm. Before I can get out of the car, his hands are on me, sliding up my thigh and under my skirt. One finger is thrust inside me, and my head falls back with a groan.

"Cars can be very dangerous, *mia regina.*" His finger curls before pulling out and being replaced by two. I whimper, grabbing his shoulder as he hovers over me. "I would hate for us to crash. You're lucky I got us home."

His fingers move quickly in and out of me. As I moan, his other hand clamps over my mouth. When he adds his thumb to massage a sensitive part of my core, I squirm and buck my hips under him.

"My job is to protect you, *mia regina*. You made that very hard by making *me* very hard." My stomach tightens the same as it did last night before I peaked in pleasure. My legs shake and my heartbeat is in my core, beating against his fingers. "So, you're going to cum right here. Then we're going to go to our home, and you'll do it again."

His hand over my mouth is replaced with his lips. He bites my lower lip, sucking on it as he plays with me. I wiggle and squirm and thrust my hips. Noè doesn't relent. My body cries for him, and in an instant, I am undone. My legs shake and my core clenches around his fingers. As my body falls from its high, his pace slows, and his lips leave mine.

"Good girl. Now go into our home and get naked for me."

"I don't often like to follow orders," I remind him, breathless.

"But you will," Noè challenges.

"For you, *mio re*."

CHAPTER 22

Adelaide Bendoni

Dressed in gold and black, Noè and I decided to spend our evening in one of the less busy lounges. Card players occupied a few of the tables. Smoke filled the room along with the gentle playing of a piano. We sat and Noè got us drinks from the bar. The place was more slow-paced, perfect for those who want to drink and relax after a long day. City councilmen and other officials frequented here, knowing it was a safe space for them to have a smoke and drink while they relaxed. Mostly men, but a few females lined the room as well.

I wince as I sit, my body still sore and sensitive from our afternoon together. Noè had me finish three times before we were done. The first in the car, then twice around his cock.

We bathed together before deciding to have dinner with Nonno and Beth. Felix came with us to the house but told me my normal overnight security would be foregone since I was married now. Noè seemed happy with that. It means they trust him to protect me, should Cristiano come for me again. However, three of my men circled the room now, not trusting the clubs anymore since at attack on Friday.

I spoke to a few of my men as Noè retrieved us drinks, and rumors of my husband already spread. Those at the warehouse this morning passed on what they witnessed to their friends, who told their friends.

Noè sat beside me on the velvet sofa, passing me a glass of wine. I share what I've heard with him. "They said that man died slowly and painfully from this morning. Said he choked on his own blood," I inform Noè. "They say you soaked your hands with blood."

"First day on the job, I had to make an impression."

"That you did," I say, reaching for his hand.

"Are you mad that his death was slow?"

"No, you made your point. He threatened me and insulted me, no one will do that in front of you again."

"And if they do when I'm not there, I expect to know so I can handle it."

"I can handle myself," I remind him. "Di Pietro told me when I first took over, I'd have to get blood on my hands."

"And it will make me look bad if you have to again," he tells me. Tradition. Even though we don't follow it exactly, even though our entire relationship is nontraditional. Men protect and defend their wives. Even more so in the mafia. My men wouldn't care much, they know who I am. But the other bosses would see Noè as weak if I had to defend myself.

"You want to be my enforcer?" I tease him.

"I want to be anything you need me to be." He kisses my forehead. We relax into one another, letting the slow piano music wash over us. Peace. I find peace in this man. I find peace in the decisions I've had to make that lead me here. I can be angry at how those decisions were made. I can be angry at my parents for sending me away when I was young. Or I can be angry that being a woman makes me less men. But I can't find it in me to be angry at whatever forces brought me to him.

We have comfortable conversation for the rest of the evening. Talking about his family and mine, we want to take a trip down to Monticello so he can meet the man and women who raised me. I'll meet his father soon, when Cristiano brings him here, but Noè wants to take me to New York to meet his mother, brother, and cousins.

In New York, he helped manage the gun trade and imports of firearms. While we have the firearm trade in Chicago, it isn't big. Most of the guns we get are kept in the organization. Noè want to expand this, use it as a secondary income in case the lounges are ever closed because of prohibition.

We talk about moving back into Nonno's house after our honeymoon. In his will, the house will be mine when he dies, meaning as my husband, it will be Noè's. Nonno and Nonna raised their four children in that house, now all dead. My parents raised Angelo in the house, and after calling it home for three years, I want to raise mine there.

The night went on. We drank and chatted, played cards with some of the regular guests. Noè proved to be a worthy opponent at the betting table. Towards the end of the night, I picked up some of the books from the back office to take home with me. Noè and I are both ready to retreat to seclusion in our small apartment.

He waits for me in the doorway as I rummage thought the unkept office. "Remind me to get on Cory's ass for this office. It is an abomination."

"Of course, *mia regina*."

"Unacceptable," I huff, eventually finding last month's books and inventory.

Noè chuckles, taking the books from me. We start to leave the office, only to be stopped by Luca. His jaw is tight, and eyebrows set in a line.

"Boss," he greets me, then turning to Noè. His eyes widen and shift between us. Confusion spreads over his face along with panic. He doesn't know who he answers too.

"What is it, Luca?" I finally ask.

"Um, uh," he stutters. "There has been an incident. Frankie was found floating this evening."

"Floating?" Noè speaks up.

"Yes, sir. Tied to one of the docks, drowned."

"Just Frankie?" One of the dock boys, younger but eager.

"Yes, ma'am."

"Have you fished him out?"

"Yes, ma'am."

"What do we think happened?"

"Someone drowned him, then tied him to the dock for us to find."

"The Irish?" Noè guesses.

"No, if this was recourse for those boys dying, it wouldn't have been a simple dock boy killed. It had to be personal to him," I reply before ordering Luca. "Look into his life outside us. Someone had to be targeting him for a reason."

"Yes, ma'am," Luca nods his head. "Have a good evening, ma'am. Boss." He says the last word to Noè, affirming what everyone outside of Chicago will see. Noè runs this city now, not me. The Sanna name is done, but our blood will still be here. My blood. The legacy will continue through me.

"If it isn't the Irish, I'm sure it's nothing," Noè assures me, placing his hand on my back.

"Me too, we are just tense from this whole Cristiano business. Waiting for him to come back and all." A kiss is pressed to my forehead.

"Let's go home, darling."

The streets are quiet at this time of night, and we walk back to our solitude. The apartment is only a few blocks from this longue. Hand in hand, we make our way down two blocks and over four. Drunks stumble out of other speakeasies as we walk the street. Monday nights were usually less busy for many of the alcohol sellers, but a few still kept a crowd on the weekdays. As a few men stumble from an alley, Noè pulls me closer, releasing my hand and wrapping his arm around me instead.

Back in our bedroom, we undress in silence for bed. I take off my black gloves, my golden headpiece, and my beaded dress. Pins are removed from hair and the brown curls are released down to my shoulders. I wash the makeup off my face and re-dress in a simple nightgown of cream silk. As I finish, I find Noè waiting for me in bed. He's shirtless, preferring to sleep only in a simple pair of pajama pants.

I smile at the sight of him. His blonde hair falling over his face while he settles in the sheets. My husband. The only man I would want to go to bed to, and I get to every night. I walk around the bed, so I'm standing by his side. Noè reaches up, placing a hand on my hip. I touch his cheek, stroking my thumb over his skin.

"Come to bed, darling," Noè coos to me.

I crawl onto my husband, straddling his lap. His other hand reaches for me as well, so both his hands are on me. I lean over and kiss him, dragging my tongue over his lips.

"I enjoy going to bed with you," I whisper to him.

"Un piacere per me, mia regina." And then I am on my back.

CHAPTER 23

Noè Bendoni

The moon shone thought the window as I wake up. My cock hard from Addy's ass pushing against me, wiggling back and forth. She's asleep, but her hands are clenched around the sheets. Her face twitches and her hips push into me more. Addy's lips part and a soft moan comes from them. As her hips grind against me, her nightdress rides up, presenting her bare bottom to me. My arm, already resting over her middle, moves to caress her hip.

She squirms, whispering my name in her sleep. The sight of her has me chuckling and I smirk at my insatiable queen. Asleep and dreaming of all the pleasure we have together, I find it adorable. My hand slides across her stomach, down to her center. Addy shifts from her side to her back unconsciously, her legs sprawling out for me. My fingers slip down, feeling the wetness of her core.

I start massaging her lightly, playing with

her while I lean into her ear and whisper, "Darling, wake up." Addy hums, her hips rolling into my hands. I kiss her ear, licking her neck below it then blowing on her skin. She shivers, stirring at the sensation. "Addy, I need you to wake up."

Her hand covers mine over her core as her eyes open. The *sirenetta* besides me uses her free hand to reach for my cock, stroking it gently and moaning.

"You were dreaming, *reginetta*," I whisper to her. "Tell me about it."

"I need you," she begs, turning to kiss me. As much as it pains me, I deny her the kiss.

"Tell me about your dream," I still whisper, but this time make it clear that this is a demand, not an offer. Her hand grips my length, almost making me falter on my plans.

"Kiss me." Addy strokes me harder. I groan this time, taking her hand away from my cock.

"Tell me first." I lace our hands together, preventing her from going back for my cock, but keeping one of my hands free to continue stroking her nub.

"You were kissing me," she whines, frustrated at the slow pace I'm using.

"Yes, and?" I tease her. She pushes me over to my back, before climbing on top of me. Her hands pressing onto my chest for balance.

"It was like this," she says. I relax back under her, letting her be in control of the reenactment. I'd never taken a woman this way before, but the burning in her eyes intrigued me. She grabs my member again, this time sliding down on it. I groan, gipping her hips as she starts to move up and down.

"Just like this?" I growl as she leans over to kiss my chest before sucking one of my nipples.

"Yes," she hisses while her hips bob up and down on me. Her lips meet mine and our tongues play. Addy moans against my mouth, her pace increasing up and down. My cock throbs inside her, pleasure coursing through my stomach. "Touch me."

"Where?" I growl. She takes my hand and directing it to her center. I move my thumb to her clit, circling it once. Her walls squeeze my cock in a hot, wet answer. She continues kissing and nipping at my neck and ear. She squeezes me again as I stroke her clit and my ball draw up and tighten. I find myself finishing inside my wife. His nails dig into my skin, and she cries out finding her own happy ending in our midnight romp.

She lays against my chest, breathless.

"You woke me up before that part."

"I apologize for that." I run my fingers through her hair, brushing her dark curls.

"It was better awake." Addy places a light kiss on my jaw, then moving off me to lay at my side. Her eyes flutter closed and her breathing calms.

"Go back to sleep, *mia regina*."

"They were found like this," Luca tells me as we walk into one of the warehouses on the south side of Chicago. In the rafters, three boys hung by ropes. I came alone to the scene, leaving Addy with her grandfather who refused to get out of bed.

"Cut them down." Two others get up on ladders to get the boys' bodies. "What happened?"

"We don't know yet, but they work here overnight as security. When the morning shift came in, they were found dead."

"Anything stolen?"

"No, sir."

"So, someone came in, killed the security, and left without stealing anything?"

"It appears that way."

"Why would they do that?"

"If I may," Luca starts. The bodies are laid out on the ground; their eyes are closed by the two that cut them down. I nod for Luca to continue. "It may be related to Frankie yesterday."

"How so?"

"You just came into power here. It could be someone trying to test you, sir. See what they can get away with. Transitions of power are a great time to cause trouble. A similar thing happened when the boss took over."

"There were murders when she took over?" Di Pietro never told me that.

"No, there were robberies. Some of the guys stole from her because they saw her as an easy target, when she found them and punished them, it all stopped. Miss Sanna earned everyone's respect."

"Who says they don't respect me?" I ask next. "Obviously you've heard whispers of displeasure with my new leadership."

"For some," he starts cautiously. "Feels wrong that you took over. Feels like a large power grab by the Bendoni family."

"My father owns this country," I remind him. "The American head of the mafia."

"And some want to see you weakened," Luca adds. "Some never liked Miss Sanna's job as boss here and see this as a way to break down your family and hers. Some that still support her cousin."

"I assume you know who would want to do that?"

He nods slowly, looking around to see who is cleaning up the mess left by the bodies, "I have suspicions."

"Look into it, make a list, bring it to me this afternoon at the house. I also want to know who these men were so I can let their families know what has happened," I say and Luca nods. They were all very young, probably without a wife. But their mothers and fathers will want to know they've died. If this is happening because of me, then I'll find whoever killed these boys and the one from yesterday and end them myself.

The idea that after all she's done for this city that there are those that still challenge her capability makes my blood boil. As Luca said, she earned all their loyalty three years ago. I understood when I married her that I too would have to earn their loyalty, but murdering our men to test me went too far. These people are traitors, and they will pay. An example had to be made here like it was with the Irish.

"Is there anything else I should know?" I ask Luca as we walk out of the warehouse.

"Yes." We stop outside the car I drove here. Luca, in all his massiveness, stood taller and wider than me. "I am loyal to Adelaide Sanna first, if you hurt her, I don't care who your father is, I will kill you."

I smirk, "Noted."

"Many of the men feel the same as me."

"But not all, obviously."

"Not all, but enough of us."

"Thank you for looking out for her."

With that, I enter the car and drive away from the warehouse. Something still not sitting right with me about the murders. Frankie was drowned yesterday and this morning there are three hangings. It doesn't feel like a test against me. I'd been tested before. Before my padre let me join the business, he had me kidnapped and tortured for three days. No food, naked in a warehouse in a New York winter, bleeding from cut marks all over my body. He gave me no warning, no one did. I had thought it was the Irish or the Russians at first. When I escaped and made it home, he welcomed me into the business with a handshake. Apparently, Elio went through the same thing before he could work for padre too, it had taken him a week to escape.

This was not a test; this was blatant betrayal. Someone wanted to distract us with the murders. Keep our resources looking at our own people instead of at the outside. It had Cristiano's name written all over it.

Addy sat with her secretary, Irene, in the parlor when I got to the house on Gold Coast. I kissed her cheek when I entered and sat in a plush chair by the window. "How is Nonno?"

"Still in bed, but Beth and I got him to eat something at least," she sighs. "The warehouse?"

"Three dead, nothing stolen that we know of, although they had opportunity. I still think it is Cristiano."

"This could have to do with the rat that went to the police about our shipment," Irene offers.

"The rat could be a mascot for Cristiano," Addy says with another sigh, her hands folded tightly in her lap. Her fingers start to turn white from the force and a part of me urges to take her hands and comfort her. I resist, wanting to keep up appearances even if it is just Irene watching. When we are alone later, I'll hold her hand and kiss away the crease in her brow. "They are obviously trying to get to us. Irene, get Titone and Ranzi here."

She stands and nods, "What should I tell them?"

"That I need them."

Irene leaves to do as my wife bids. Addy's phone is in her office, so no doubt that is where she'll go to make the calls. As we sit alone in the parlor, I move to be at her side on the couch.

"He isn't doing well, is he?"

"He isn't speaking, not even to me, not even in Italian." Her head of soft curls rests gently on my shoulder. "I don't know what to do once he's gone. Three years I've had to plan for it, but I still don't know."

"You won't be alone," I assure her. "I will be with you."

CHAPTER 24

Adelaide Bendoni

"When will Cristiano be back?" Titone asks as we gather in the parlor. Irene sat in the corner, while Titone and Renzi sat in the chairs across from myself and Noè. Di Pietro was still on bed rest from his gunshot wound, so Irene would defer any decisions made back to him. "And if another Bendoni is coming to town, we need to be better prepared this time."

The older men glare at my husband. "We will be. I want security increased at all my warehouses. Cancels shipments until Bettino Bendoni and Cristiano return and we can stop these killings," I say, taking the attention off Noè.

"You should stay here too, protected," Renzi suggests which earns him a scowl from me.

"So, I get married and suddenly I'm in need of protecting," I growl at the underboss of inventory. "I'll do and go as I please."

"Cristiano is out for blood. I wouldn't put it

past him to order whoever he hired that they could kill you if they get the chance," Renzi argues. "Di Pietro should have killed him years ago."

"And it was my father's order that stopped him, not mine," I remind sharply.

"Of course,' Renzi replied tensely.

"She will be safe," Noè assures them. "And Cristiano will pay for this. My father will come here and do all the formalities that are necessary, then he will leave us be."

"What about the murders? I can't lose half my dock workers to this feud," Renzi directed to Noè. These two men don't yet trust him, they' re waiting to see if the *principe* can be a *re*.

"As my wife said, more security, cancel shipments, and have the men go places in pairs," he answers. "Let's also merge the warehouses, close out some of them and use them as decoys. Keep normal security at the empty warehouses and double it at the ones we fill."

"I'll have my father send the men," Irene stands from her spot. "Do you need anything else?"

"I'll go with you," I stand from the couch. "I want to check on Di Pietro."

"Luca should go with you," Noè reminds me. We spoke earlier while they gathered about protection for both of us. Noè is good with guns and proved good at protecting himself during the years in New York, but he promised to keep Felix by his side when out in public. The same way I've proven myself over the years. I'm smart, and my smarts keep me out of trouble and safe. And being smart means keeping Luca nearby when I'm out in public. I won't let my advisors tell me to stay put and be quiet. I won't be a soft mafia wife. Noè and I agree though, we'd keep a bodyguard close to stay safe.

I nod to Noè, kissing his cheek before leaving the house with Irene. Luca sat outside on the porch with Felix. When we walk out, he stands ready to follow us. We start down the street, Luca three paces behind.

"Doriano's black eye is better," Irene says as we start. "And papa is making a good recovery. He asked how you and Mr. Bendoni are doing? So, I thought I'd check in with it?"

"We're doing great," I say with a slight blush. "We're enjoying our alone time, but with all that is happening with Cristiano and Nonno... We're going to move back into the house sooner than we hoped."

"How is your Nonno?"

"He's gone more often than he's here," I admit, the giddy feeling in my gut from a moment ago is now gone. "We'll lose him soon."

"I'm sorry, Addy. I know how much you care for your Nonno."

"It's alright, because I was scared to be alone before and now, I'm not going to be alone." Having Noè in my life, while unplanned and unexpected, it is a relief in a time like this. He is a strength and a comfort.

"You were never going to be alone," Irene promises me, grabbing my hand and resting it in her elbow. The streets are fairly quiet for the afternoon. A few cars on the road, some children playing with a street cat. By the sound of its cries, they're tormenting the poor pussycat. "You will always have me."

"Thank you, but it is different now. You're a dear friend to me, but he is my husband," I try to explain how it feels now. Before, when Nonno died I expected to be alone. The mafia is a family, and the men here are like my brothers and cousins. Still, in the house, alone. I would have no one. No one to come home too, no one to eat meals with daily. Irene didn't spend every waking minute here like she did before she was married. Maybe before she was married it would be different. I was so happy for my friend when she walked the aisle, but I was also saddened by the fact that she wouldn't be around as much. I add, "He can never get rid of me."

Irene laughs at this. "That is true. Vows are till death you do part." A young couple passes us with a pram, the baby slept quietly inside.

"He is being very supportive. I hope it doesn't change after his father's visit."

"Bendoni seems like a good man. My father thinks he will be good to you. Plus, it is in his eyes, he obviously loves you."

"What?" I look at my friend wide eyed. Noè is very supportive and caring, but love? Love is something I never imagined myself having with a husband. Any marriage I made was always meant to be about power and politics. I love my Nonno, I plan to love my children, but it never occurred to me that I might love my husband.

Devoted? Yes. Caring? Of course. Supportive? Obviously. But nothing more than an obligation. Something I'd share with a business partner. In my mind, any husband of mine would be like another advisor. Like Renzi, Titone, and Di Pietro, but less fatherly.

"You're wrong," I tell Irene. "He does not love me."

"He very clearly does." A radio blares from one of the houses we pass, drawing my attention momentarily.

"You cannot know that," I counter, because she couldn't know it. Not even if it is true, which it is not.

"I can. It is the way he looks at you, like you are the last ray of sunlight left on earth. He is in love with you."

"He can't be," I breathe out. "It is dangerous for both of us that way."

Loving makes you reckless with your decisions. It makes you do things you wouldn't otherwise do. It makes you lose common sense and act without thinking. It makes you a fool. Noè is no fool.

"I personally am happy for you. I always hoped you'd find someone who loved you for you and not your position." We turn the corner onto the block of her parent's home. I see it off in the distance.

"How do you know it is not my position he loves?"

We stop and she takes both my hands, "Because you are standing in this street with me now and not locked away in your house. Because when you laugh, he smiles and when you are upset, he frowns. Because he entered your marriage receiving nothing in return for saving you."

"You're right." I feel emotion rise into my eyes as I think about it. He does love me.

A car drives by us. A shot rings out in the air, and I instantly duck down. Luca lunges to my side, trying to block me from the street. Warm blood covers my face and chest. I gasp at the feeling of it. Luca is speaking to me, but I barely hear it. I try to feel my body, feel where the blood is coming from.

Nothing hurts.

Nothing... hurts?

CHAPTER 25

Noè Bendoni

"**S**he needs more protection than Luca," Renzi says once my wife leaves.

"She will be fine," I assure him, frowning at him. I never expected anyone to treat her differently once we were married. Yet, it seems her underboss wants her to take the position of docile mafia wife. A part that Addy will never play. "Di Pietro's home is not far."

A few blocks, and Luca will call when they arrive. When I told her I wanted the enforcer with her anytime I wasn't, she pushed back at first. I reminded her that it was that way for three years before our wedding and it eased her anger. My wife was no fragile queen and hates to be treated as if she is. It surprises me that Renzi hasn't realized this yet.

"When do you think your father will be here?" Titone asks, changing our subject. He pours three glasses of bourbon and passes them out.

"Soon, I'd wager," I say, taking the glass.

"Does your father like you?" Titone asks next. "I mean, if he doesn't like you and places Cristiano in her seat, then the marriage will be for nothing."

"My father likes me more than he likes Cristiano Sanna," I assure him with a sharp glare. Our marriage is not pointless. "What needs discussing is the murders that have been happening in the warehouses. Renzi, you're in charge of these areas, what is happening?"

"We're not sure, but it must be Cristiano's doings."

"Well, find out. The men that die in those warehouses are your responsibility and if the killing doesn't stop then you will be held accountable," I warn him. I can tell Addy is equally upset by the murders as I am. They need to stop. Her solution is increased security and mine is to find the *verme* that is getting our men killed. Renzi is supposed to be in charge of the warehouses, and these murders make him incompetent in my mind.

"You blame me for this?"

"I don't blame Titone, that's for sure. You should know that with all that is happening your security needs increasing without my wife telling you. We've had shipments stolen and men killed. All on your watch. Yes, I blame you for this. Cristiano may have ordered the kills and the robberies, but the warehouses should be better maintained that he had no opportunity to kill or steal."

"I will do better, sir," Renzi says through gritted teeth.

"Good, now go." He leaves. Titone sits across from me with inquisitive eyes. "What?"

"You think he's untrustworthy."

"I have seen nothing to contradict it."

"Tread lightly, your wife actually cares for that man."

"Do you trust him?"

"I trust Miss Sanna, she is my boss. She's the only one I trust fully." Meaning he doesn't really trust me either.

"That is good. I like a suspicious man."

"Renzi can be too big for himself sometimes. He wants to be close to Miss Sanna like Di Pietro is, but he never will be. That makes him angry."

"Angry enough to betray us?"

Titone shrugs, standing from his seat. "That's for you to discover on your own."

CHAPTER 26

Adelaide Bendoni

Luca keeps grabbing me, keeps trying to assess me. I push past him, going to Irene who held her chest with a look of fear in her eyes. Her wide, beautiful eyes. I grab her shoulders, pulling her body to mine and holding her. My friend. My only real friend. Her blood stains the pretty blouse she wore today. She always dresses prettily, always so put together. I put my hand over hers, blood pooling over her fingers and onto mine.

"You're alright, you're alright," I say to her over and over again. Luca grabs my shoulder, but I brush him off. "Go call a doctor. Call someone!"

"I can't leave you here."

"Go to their house, get someone! That is an order!" I demand of him. Luca nods once and runs down the street to the Di Pietro home. He doesn't knock, just rushes inside. Two of Irene's brothers come out and run to us.

"Ad-- Addy?"

"I'm here. You're alright. Just breathe."

"Tell Dor--" she coughs and coughs and coughs. I shush to her, rocking us back and forth. Her brothers are at my sides. "I love him... tell him."

They lift her from my arms, and half run back to their house. Luca lifts me from the ground, leading me to the front door.

Inside, her mother comes down the stairs. She goes to her daughter and takes her hand. She's crying, screaming for someone to help her. One of the boys called the doctor, he's on his way. Di Pietro wobbles down to follow her. He looks over me first, then to Irene who was laid on the floor of the parlor.

Our eyes meet, and he asks me a silent question. I've seen many gunshot wounds over my three years running Chicago. After some time, it becomes easier to tell if they will survive or not. Irene won't survive this. Di Pietro taught me how to assess gunshot wounds and where to shot to make sure they die and where to shot to only inflict pain. Irene was shot in her chest, close to her heart. She'll bleed out.

He is asking me where it is, if she'll survive it the way he did. I shake my head, a small subtle movement that Mrs. Di Pietro won't clock. He grabs his wife, holding her close to him. She tries to get out of his arms, go to her injured daughter. But Di Pietro knows it's best not to get her covered in Irene's blood. She'll never get the feeling off her skin.

A doctor arrives, and he assesses Irene quickly. It only takes a minute for him to come to the same conclusion as me. Irene will die. We all stand around her, with her younger brothers holding her hands. Her eyes close, her breathing slows. One last gasp and she's gone.

Doriano arrives then, just moments after she's gone. He crumbles to the floor and gathers her into his arms. He cries for her.

"My baby," Mrs. Di Pietro cries. "She's gone. My baby,"

"I'm so sorry," I tell her. The woman who has become like a mother to me pulls me to her chest. She hugs me close, despite her daughter's blood covering me. "She was a good friend."

"No, no, no," Mrs. Di Pietro cries. She cries and begs and denies it all is happening.

Di Pietro takes his wife from me. Taking her away from the blood and the dead body. He's protected her for years from the anguish of our work. He's done right by her in keeping her and their children safe. And now the blood of our streets has poured into his parlor.

The door opens and Luca is pushed aside. My husband comes in behind me and makes me face him. Noè grabs my face, smearing the blood on my cheek.

"Are you--"

"No, it wasn't me." I turn, making him look to Doriano crying over Irene's body. "It was supposed to be me."

"Adelaide, this isn't your fault."

"No," I agree with him. "It is Cristiano's and the only one that can forgive him is God." I turn to Luca and Felix. "Spread it through the city that whoever can find the men who did this and delivers their heads will receive my greatest thanks. And if anyone brings me Cristiano's head will have my favor."

"Yes, boss," they both say before leaving.

I walk over to Doriano and the body, placing my hand on his shoulder. "She loved you dearly. She wanted you to know that."

"I know," Doriano responds. He stands from the ground, looking at me with hope in his eyes. "I'll find them for you, boss. I'll find them and kill them."

"As is your right," I tell him. "I'm so sorry for this."

"I don't blame you. I will avenge her with your grace."

"You have my full support in taking this as far as you need."

"Thank you, boss."

"Give them hell, Doriano." I take Noè's hand, finding comfort in his touch. I start for the stairs, planning to see Di Pietro before we leave. As we get to the second floor, the man steps out of the master bedroom. I can hear his wife's sobs from inside.

"Doriano cannot go after them alone," he says first.

"You cannot help him, you're still recovering," I remind him. "Doriano won't do it alone, Noè will help him."

"Your husband doesn't know this city like I do."

"He doesn't need to know this city to keep Doriano alive. You need to be with your family."

"My daughter is dead!"

"She is," I wince. "But it is Doriano who lost a wife, it is him with the strongest claim to revenge."

"She was your friend," Di Pietro reminds me. Something I didn't need reminded of, I knew who Irene was to me.

"That is why Noè is going to help him."

"Go home," Di Pietro tells me. "Go home and stay safe. We cannot lose you too."

Outside, two other enforcers wait for Noè and me. They escort us, one on either side, back to my family's home. The streets are quiet since the shooting. People are locked back in their home. Noè doesn't let go of me the entire walk. The enforcers wait outside while we go in. Beth looks over me with panic before I assure her the blood isn't mine. She offers to run me a bath and I gratefully accept.

When we are alone, Noè hugs me, he tucks my head under his chin and holds me close. My arms wrap around his mid-section, I grab his shirt and hold him with equal fervor. He strokes my head and rubs my back. I feel tears burn my eyes; tears I didn't dare shed at the Di Pietro house. I didn't want to shed them now either, I wanted to focus. There is too much to do.

"Don't leave until I'm finished cleaning myself up," I order him, but really it is a silent plea for him not to go. I can't let him leave yet. I need him here for me. I know he need to help Doriano, I promised Di Pietro that he would help. I don't want to send him out though, I don't want to risk him not coming home.

In that, I realize that he may love me, or he may not... but I love him.

"God, Addy, I was so worried. I heard the shot and didn't think too much of it until Luca called the house," he says into my hair. Noè places a kiss on my temple. "I'm so sorry Irene was killed, but I'm so relieved that it wasn't you."

"It should have been me, I'm the one they want."

"Please stay here, while Doriano and I handle this. I can't lose you and neither can this city."

"I cannot sit idle." I try to pull away from him, but my husband just holds me tighter.

"Don't be idle then, but please stay here. I don't beg often, Adelaide, but I am begging you now to stay in this house tonight."

"She was my friend," I sniffle.

"Doriano and I will bring you their heads. I promise you that. We will avenge her, blood for blood." He kisses my temple. "Go take a bath. Get her blood off you."

"Stay, until I'm done." I look up at him, his messy blonde hair that is usually perfect. His eyes bore into my soul and demand attention. Demand I stare into them and feel his gaze. Irene said his love is in his eyes. I'd looked into them many times before, but I guess I never realized. They're soft when he looks at me, but hard and analytical when he looks elsewhere.

"I'll stay," he promises me with one more kiss to my lips. "I'll bring you up something to eat. Go bathe."

So, I do. Upstairs in my bathroom, Beth has drawn me a nice bath. I scrub off the blood from my hands and face with plans to burn my clothing that is covered in it. The water turns a grotesque pink color before I drain it and dry myself. I run a comb through my curls and tie them in ribbons for the evening. I remove what is left of my makeup and wash my face with cold water.

The bedroom I've occupied for three years waits for me with my husband inside. He has a small tea tray sat at the table by the window. I don a dressing gown and sit with him. He serves me orange pekoe tea with ginger cookies and shortbreads with blackberry jam.

"I don't trust Renzi," he says to me first while pouring the tea.

"I haven't trusted him for a year. He lost a shipment last March from Vinegar Hill, and the crates turned up at different speakeasies across the city. I have Titone's son working under him to report on any misdeeds. What do you think he's doing?"

"I think he's the rat."

I look up from my tea and stare him down. "Maybe, but I have someone watching him at all times. I'd know if he was the rat."

"I want to continue looking into it," Noè says to me, and I nod to give him my blessing. "What did she say to you? Before she died? Obviously, you have something she said on your mind."

She said you loved me. I want to tell him. Now isn't the time. Now isn't the time for me to be worried about him; to fret over if he'll come home. I don't want to love him, because then it is complicated. Then I will worry anytime he's out late and anytime I send him on an errand. Then I blame myself if he's hurt and mourn if he dies. I don't want to be like Doriano crying over a bleeding body.

"*Reginetta?*"

I take his hand across the table. "She said she loved Doriano, that she wanted him to know."

"You told him. I'm sure he knows." His thumb rubs the back of my hand. "Is that all?"

I shake my head, taking a sip of tea.

"Do you not want to tell me?"

"I don't know. I don't think I want it to be real."

"We can talk about it later then. Get some rest," he stands from the small table and kisses my head. "Don't wait up, I'll be back late."

CHAPTER 27

Noè Bendoni

Rain started to pour by the time I returned to my wife that night. A light drizzle that soaked deep with how long I've walked the streets. Doriano and I spend the first hour with Luca, going over every step of the walk. He was able to catch the car plate that the gun was fired from. We took that number to one of Addy's police contacts to find out who owned the car. We tracked that back to an old man named Harris Wentworth, a man almost seventy years old with no living relatives. So, it became a dead end.

From his home, we looked into his staff: two maids and a nurse. Nothing suspicious there, nothing tying them to the Irish or Cristiano. After all that, we hit the street to investigate the hit and what the organization is saying about it. Doriano showed me the underbelly of the city tonight, places he says Di Pietro won't let Addy go, for fear of her safety. Back alleys, smoke rooms, and the dirtiest of speakeasies serving the most rancid liquor.

The late afternoon and evening left me smelling bad, half drunk, and exhausted beyond what was normal. I found myself stripping in the bathroom, doing a quick wash in the tub with semi-cold water, and climbing into bed.

As I pulled back the covers, Addy stirs from her sleep. I settle into my side of the bed, while Addy also moves onto my side of the bed. She molds herself to my side, resting her head on my shoulder.

"Any progress?" she asks with a yawn.

"A little, not much. I told Doriano to go home and get some sleep and we'd continue in the morning," I inform her, my hand running up and down the length of her back.

"How is he?"

Numb. Ready to kill anyone and everyone. Ready to kill himself once his revenge is done. "Grieving."

I couldn't image being where he is now. Losing my wife, losing Addy, it would leave me worse than where Doriano is right now. He wants his pound of flesh, but he also doesn't want to live without her. He loves her. Love, which doesn't always happen within mafia marriages. Di Pietro told me in a letter that Doriano married his daughter to help him move up in the mafia. He was a warehouse worker before their wedding, and now he's a manager of three, directly under Renzi. He grew to love Irene in their time married. It will take time for him to grieve for his wife.

If Addy had been shot, if the bullet met its target and Addy had been the one to drop, it would leave me heartbroken. I know I made him go home and sleep, but I also know if it was me, I wouldn't be able to sleep. I don't think I'll ever be able to sleep without *mia reginetta* by my side.

"Are you alright?" I ask her, trying to distract myself from the thoughts of her being hurt and dying.

"I miss her already." she admits. "It should have been me."

"No," I pull her closer. "If it had been you then it would be me alone."

"Irene didn't deserve to die."

"Many don't, but everyone does eventually. It is the nature of the job that those we care about get caught up in things they shouldn't," I try to comfort her. I don't know if I'm succeeding. In reality, I've only known my wife for a few weeks. Despite Di Pietro's letters, she is different in person. I get see the side of her that I'm sure she doesn't show others. It a part of her that reminds me she wasn't raised in this life. She was raised in a small town, to be a farmer's wife.

Now she's a mafia boss and must be cold and harsh. While I know she loves what she does, I also know it goes against part of her nature. It is a part of her personality that I've come to adore. She's a mafia boss and has all the traits of a man born to kill. Yet, she's still a woman. She's still soft and kind.

"I was prepared for Nonno's death. I wasn't prepared for her to die."

"Do you want to talk about what she said?"

Addy sighs. She sits up in bed, climbing over me and sits on my hips with her legs on either side. Her hands cup my cheeks, and she kisses me. It is slow and soft. Nothing demanding, just a kiss. Almost like she's exploring me. When she pulls away, her light eyes stare into mine, like she's looking for something. Her eyebrows furrow as she thinks.

"She said you love me."

The answer is simple, "I do."

"You love me?"

"Yes." I've loved her for a while now. I loved her through Di Pietro's letters, I loved her confidence when we first met, I loved her anger when she thought I was here to dethrone her. I love her fire and her sweetness.

I know loving her is dangerous, but I stopped caring about the danger long ago. I knew when I decided to marry her that it would come at the risk of my life, and I accepted that. Being the king of Chicago comes with many dangers, but it also came with her. Her, who I'd do anything for.

"I love you," I finally tell her, and she kisses me again. This kiss is less soft than the last. This kiss says she understands the danger I put us in by loving her. This kiss tells me she feels it too, but she's afraid to say it. Loving is a weakness in our world. It means you have too much to lose, and when your love is threatened, you'd do anything to protect it.

Addy kisses my cheek and chin and jaw. Down my neck where she nibbles and sucks. Desire for her rolls through my gut. I know what I want from her, but she's just lost her best friend.

"Addy... stop," I tell her. She licks up my neck and sucks on my ear lobe.

"I want you, Noè. *Mio re.*"

"Are you sure?" She kisses me again, biting my lip and licking it again over where her teeth were.

"Yes."

I kiss her back, letting her tongue into my mouth. I lift the hem of her nightdress, feeling her bare skin underneath. I only wore my sleeping pants, and her hand snakes down into them. She strokes my cock, making my gut twist as pleasure floods me. I groan against her lips and my little queen smirks.

"I like hearing you," she admits to me, moving to kiss my neck again. My wife squeezes me again, ever so slightly, which pulls another sound from me.

"Addy," I moan. She has to stop soon, or I'll finish without getting inside her. I reach between her tights, feeling how wet and ready she is for me. I run my fingers up her slit, caressing the small bundle of flesh at the top that makes her squirm. "I want in here."

She nods, pulling down my pants just enough to let my cock spring out. She holds it, positioning herself, but before she impales herself on me, I flip us over. I plunge into her, and the gasp from her lips only makes me harder. I let her sounds guide me to a pace that makes her pant with pleasure. My wife wraps her arms around me, digging her nails into my back.

"Yes, Noè, please..." Addy says my name, over and over with the rhythm of our hips. Almost begging me to take her to the height of her pleasure. I kiss her, licking her lips and nibbling on them. Her cries continues as I nail her into the bed.

"Noè," she mumbles onto my lips. Her legs wrap around my waist, holding me against her. My back burns as her nails break skin, but the pain only makes the pleasure sear through me faster.

Her core clenches me and she buries her face into my neck as she orgasms. I finish inside her with my own cry. Her eyes are shut tight I continue to thrust us through the orgasms, slowing ever so slightly until I'm completely still inside her. I watch her come down from her high, this is one of my favorite parts of sex with her. Watching her relax into me after finishing. She kisses me once more as I pull out.

"I love you too."

CHAPTER 28

Adelaide Bendoni

Noè leaves just after breakfast with Doriano. Leaving me alone with Nonno. I let Beth have the morning to herself while I sit with him in the parlor, reading to him from his Bible. I pick up in Psalms, where Beth last left of for him. I don't fully understand the Italian in it, but I can pronounce it well enough that Nonno seems content. He smiles and nods along as though he understands. After about forty minutes he starts to nod off. I successfully get him up the stairs and into his bed. He sleeps more and more recently, making me think the more he sleeps the closer we are to his death.

Instead of sleeping in the Master bedroom, Nonno sleeps in the one closest to the stairs. It makes it easier having him near the stairs to get him up and down them. The Master bedroom still sits empty since my father died and it never felt right taking up the room for myself. With Noè's father coming, we'll let him have the room. It will make him feel important.

I prepare the room for a guest. Cleaning off the dust and making the bed, I can't help but feel useless. This is my city, my family, and my legacy. Yet, I've been confined to this house for my own protection. My husband is out there helping avenge my best friend, and all I can do is clean a room and make a bed. It is pathetic.

Down in the office, I check my books. Noè expressed a distrust in Renzi. He took a long time to warm up to me when I first took over. So, when a shipment went missing, my first guess was him. However, he always played a loyal man around Titone and Di Pietro. I still watched him closely and had Titone's son spying on him regularly. Of course, Titone and Di Pietro didn't know I kept my eyes on him, and if they did, they never mentioned it.

Now that Noè didn't trust him either, it gave me an excuse to look over the warehouse inventories again. We had one shipment go missing that I know of, but if Renzi really is backstabbing me, there will be more missing inventory. He would have made too much off those crates to not do it again. The taste of that money would be too great for any man to deny having again.

I've always double checked these books myself every couple of months. So, any inconsistencies should have been caught before now. Either way, I check them again. All the numbers look right, but I pull the longue books to compare inventory received to that sold. Eight lounges now, and nothing looks wrong with the numbers. Meaning if Renzi is stealing from me, he's got the longue managers in on it. I just don't see that as happening. I don't see him having that many of my men in his pocket.

"Luca," I call out, knowing he's just on the porch. The front door opens and closes before he comes into the office. His large frame looms in the doorway.

"Yes, boss?"

"Renzi, do people like him?"

"He's a hard ass, very strict on the dock workers. I heard Mr. Bendoni ripped him a new one about the murders and the missing inventory from this week. He's apparently working his staff overtime to figure out what's happening. As for liking him? No. The men under him respect him and do as he says."

"If he needed to make inventory disappear, would they do that for him?"

Luca's eyes darken at what I'm suggesting, and he shakes his head. "No."

"How do you figure that?"

"Renzi was one of your father's men, so they know what he was like under your father. They know that they're getting paid more now than they were before and that was at your discretion, not his. Their hours are less than they were before, that is all you. They know who to be loyal too."

"Is Felix with my husband?"

"Yes."

"Where are they?"

"Felix heard of a lead they are following on the south side of the city. The car that the gunman used lead nowhere, so they're working a few rumors that are on the street."

"Is there any word on my cousin?"

"No, there is nothing yet on Cristiano's whereabouts."

I sigh, closing the books with all the mind-numbing numbers in them. I stand and look Luca up and down. "We're going to the warehouses. I want to see each of them."

"Boss, Mr. Bendoni told me you should stay here."

"Luca, I'm going to go crazy sitting here."

"I'd rather you go crazy than get killed, boss. Plus, if I let anything happen to you Mr. Bendoni will have my head. I'm sure it won't be a fun death either, he'll make it hurt."

"You should be more afraid of me going crazy than of my husband." With that, I push past him to grab my shoes. "He won't hurt you as long as I have a say in it."

"And it will be open season if you die."

"Beth will be heading back soon to take care of Nonno. Luca, I want to go to the warehouses. I don't care if you need to bring a whole gaggle of men with us, so you feel better about it. We are going."

Ten minutes later, Beth arrived, and Luca and I left. Luca drove, and two young men sat in the back of the car, terror written across their faces. On short notice, I'm sure Luca summoned the closest two guards available, and judging on how scared they look. It is clear that they've never been near me before. Or anyone high up in our organization. They're fresh meat.

We spent the morning in three warehouses. Their managers give me tours with shaky hands. I don't often visit the warehouses. I am more involved with the lounges and rely on more second-hand accounts of our imports.

At lunch, I visit one of the lounges that act more like an upscale restaurant. One of the ones my father built during his time in the city. He proposed to my mother in this restaurant. It became one of the first fronts for bootlegging when prohibition hit. A nice glass of brandy or bourbon with meals was an easy way to get city officials into our pockets.

Luca sat across from me stoic as I reviewed some of my notes from the warehouses. "The dock areas seem to be too easily accessible. Who owns the docks beside ours?"

"I'm not sure," Luca replies, his head on a swivel.

"And that broken window on the Fulton Street warehouse needs fixed. How long has it been broken?"

"I don't know." He isn't paying me any

mind. Instead, Luca watches every person in the immediate vicinity. He trusts no one around me. In his mind, Cristiano will pop out at any moment and slit my throat.

"Do you wish for me to return home?"

"Yes," Luca stands. "Let's return."

"Luca, sit," I growl at him, and he follows my order. "I am not a dame."

"No but you have a price on your head. Please, let's go back." I continue my glare at him and the large man squirms under my scrutiny. "I know you're not a dame. Hell, I know you're not delicate or any other word that I would use to describe most ladies. You're my boss though, and I want to keep you safe and alive. It is dangerous for you to be out right now. If you wish it, I will go to the rest of the warehouses for you and rip every one of their asses. Please, go home."

I know he's right. I know that my life is in danger and Cristiano wants me dead. I know that I'm in a tight spot and need to be safe. Yet, I also cannot sit in that house and do nothing to avenge Irene. I need to feel like there is something I can do to return my city to normal operations and protect the rest of my men.

Protect Noè.

Because if I lose my husband, I don't know what I'll do. Still, the people close to me are hurting. Noè, Doriano, and Di Pietro were all attacked by men trying to get to me. Irene was killed by a bullet meant for me. My dock workers are being killed for no damn reason.

I nod to Luca, standing from my seat and allowing him to take me home.

CHAPTER 29

Noè Bendoni

Addy is not home when I arrive back. Beth said she went out with Luca and two other men. I grumble as I walk up the stairs, intent on a warm bath. She shouldn't have left, and I will make sure to express my displeasure in this when she gets home. I take a hot bath, warming my body from the cold drizzle outside. It started to drip down right as Doriano, and I drug a suspect into the dungeon warehouse. The same room where I killed the men that attacked us. The man confessed quickly, naming two co-conspirators. I left Doriano to kill the man as he sees fit. Tomorrow, we will go get the two others he named and end them as well.

Hopefully with their deaths, the threat to Addy will reduce until Cristiano comes to town.

The thought of my wife somehow summons her into the room. She brings her vanity chair to the tub and sits by my head. Addy places a soft kiss on my forehead before running her fingers through my blonde hair.

"We found him," I tell her. My eyes closed as I enjoy the feeling of *mia regina*'s hands massaging my head.

"Felix told me." She kisses my head again. "Thank you." We relax in a comfortable silence. I finish my bath and as I stand to get out Addy hands me a towel. I dress in casual clothing before sitting on the bed. Addy watches me from the corner of the room. I raise my eyebrow at her before summoning her to me with a finger.

She stands between my legs, resting her hands on my shoulders. "You left."

"I needed to do something. I took Luca with me."

My chest tightens when I think of her out on the streets alone. She wasn't alone though, she took Luca with her like we discussed, and I took Felix with me. Still, I didn't want her to leave while Doriano and I hunted the *stronzo* that killed Irene and had gunned for Addy.

"I know I can't lock you in this house, but I would if I thought you wouldn't kill me for it," I tell her. Yet, I know she can't live that way, not after how she's lived the past three years. I will never change her, and I never want to.

"Luca was terrified you'd kill him if anything happened to me," she smiles.

"Then I'm doing my job correctly," I chuckle before she kisses me.

"Let's go to a club tonight," Addy suggests.

"Addy, that's--"

"There will always be danger. When it isn't Cristiano, it will be the police, or Irish mob, or Bratva. There will never be an end to the danger. We will always be worried for each other," Addy kisses me again. Reminding me why love in a mafia marriage is so dangerous. "Tonight, let's go out and remind this city that it is ours to rule."

"I cannot deny you, dear."

Addy smiles, "You cannot. *Sono la tua regina.*" *I am your queen.* She really is my queen. The only woman I will bow too, the only one I will worship.

"*Davvero?*" I ask back with a sly grin, teasing her.

"*Veramente, mio re.*" Addy kisses my cheek.

"*Ti amo, Adelaide Bendoni.*"

"*Ti amo, Noè Bendoni.*"

After dinner and putting her nonno to bed, Addy and I left for her clubs. We plan to visit three tonight, the three I have yet to see in my two weeks in Chicago. We start at a piano club, much like *Claudia.* Tonight, a violinist accompanied the piano player in the middle of the room. One of the bartenders bring us drinks as we sit in the far corner of the club. Felix and Luca, along with several other bodyguards line the room. However it is a quiet night, and the club is barely full.

"Thank you for coming to the clubs with me, dear," Addy says with a smile. She takes my hand in hers, caressing it with her thumb.

"As if I'd let you go alone," I reply.

We listen to the music, occasionally chatting about non-serious things. Watching her laugh after everything she's been through fills my heart and pride fills my chest knowing it is I that made her laugh. Before long, we leave and go to another one of her clubs. This one is fuller, with people dancing to the jazz music that echos through the hall. Addy gives me a sly grin and drags me to the middle of the floor.

It reminds me of before we were married, when my *sirena* first danced with me. Her body pressed against mine as we danced to the jazz music around us. She's closer to me now than she was when we first met. Bolder with where her hands roam now that she knows what is beneath my clothing. She's a good dancer, I learned this before. But now, she is a bit clumsier, bumping into me as we dance to the music. Her hands grazing every part of my body.

"Addy," I growl in her ear as someone bumps into her, pressing all her feminine curves to my body. One of her curls falls from the pins in her hair, dropping in front of her face. I brush it away, before kissing her forehead. Her hand squeezes my hip.

"Ten minutes?"

"Ten minutes before what?"

"If we slip away, it will be ten minutes before we're missed," she says into my neck. Desire runs through my body and straight to my cock.

"Where?"

She smirks at me, leading me away from the middle of the room. We walk behind the bar and into a back hall. There are a few bartenders and waiters that come back and forth from the storage room, but we pass them. She takes me up a narrow staircase and into a manager's office. A fat man sat behind the desk.

"Boss," he stands to greet her, then he sees me and his face furrows in confusion. "And Boss?"

"Leave, Allen. I need a moment with my husband," Addy orders him in her scary mafia boss voice. One I know all the men respect. He gives me a sympathetic look before scampering out of the office. Addy slams the door closed, locking it. When she turns to me that scary stoic look on her face is replaced with a coquettish grin.

CHAPTER 30

"Y**ou're** a devil," he tells me, stalking closer to me. My heart skips a beat at the sight of my husband ready to devour me in the office of our club. "That pour man was scared to death."

"He left though," I shrug. In a second, our lips meet in a messy display of our desire. My core throbs as pleasure courses through me. We mold together, and I feel his hard length against my stomach. I reach for his buttons, undoing his trousers and reaching my hand down them. I caress his length through his briefs. He groans against my lips, and I nibble on his lower one. He's been letting me explore touching him more the past few days and helping me learn how to touch him that makes it feel good.

I pull his trousers down slightly so his briefs can follow, freeing his cock for me to see. My hand wraps around it, stroking it as his tongue strokes against mine in my mouth. I run my thumb over his tip before giving him another thrust of my hand.

"God help me, Adelaide," he groans before taking my earlobe into his mouth and sucking on it. He reaches for the hem of my dress, and I smirk. The moment he realized I forewent my knickers for a long camisole instead results in a low rumble in his chest. Noè drags one finger between my folds, resting on the part of my core that brings me the most pleasure.

He spins us, walking us back so my bare butt rests on the desk. My dress and camisole bunch around my hips. I position his cock at my entrance, ready for him to be inside me. He moves his hand out of the way, grabs my hips, and thrusts inside me. His pace is harsh and quick, but I love it. I wrap my legs around him, digging my heals into his thighs. It restricts how much he can pull out of me, making him slide deeper and deeper with every thrust.

I moan his name, and we kiss to keep both our cries at bay. My core clenches and quivers as I know I'm climbing the hill of my pleasure. I whimper against his lips, then moan as waves of pleasure crash over me, throwing me into a climax. I bite down on Noè's lower lip, riding out the crest of the hill. He groans, thrusting deep in me as he finds his own pleasure.

Noè pants, resting his forehead against mine. "Have I used my full ten minutes?"

"I don't," I gasp for a breath. "Think so."

He gives me a final small kiss as he pulls out. I think we're done but he kneels in front of me. I watch him curiously as he kisses up my thigh, nibbling on my skin. He dips down, licking up my core before sucking. I gasp, the sensitive flesh exploding under his tongue. I grab the edges of the desk, holding on while he licks and sucks and tongues me. He laps at his own seed as it spills out, thrusting it back inside me.

"Noè!" I cry out, wanting to pull his head away and give myself a reprieve from the waves upon waves of tortuous pleasure. My head spins as my stomach tightens. I try to force my legs closed, but he holds them open with his hands, not relenting on my core. When I climax again, it rushes down my spine and through my legs. Everything shakes and it feels as though it goes on for eternity.

As he licks up the remains of our union from my core, I try to catch my breath. Every lick makes me jump and squirm, even though they're gentle. When he stands in front of me again, he fixes his trousers back together before smoothing out my hair for me. He caresses down my cheek makes me feel so cared for and loved.

"*Ti amo, mia regina,*" Noè tells me with a soft smile.

"Noè..." I lean into him. "That felt...amazing."

He chuckles, continuing to stroke my cheek. "We will have to do that more."

"*Ti amo, mio re*," I reply, kissing his cheek.

"Do you think you'll be able to walk back down to the club?"

"Absolutely not," I answer with a laugh.

"You have no one to blame but yourself, you're the one who brought me up here and didn't wear any knickers," he accuses me. We laugh together before he kisses my cheek. "You're the most beautiful after sex."

"I think you're the most handsome when you sleep," I tell him, moving my hands over his face so his eyelids flutter close.

"Boss!" Allen yells as he knocks on the door.

"Our ten minutes are up," I whisper to him.

"Sadly. But we will have all night when we get home." I stand and fix my dress. We share one last kiss before Noè opens the door. Allen stands there with wide eyes.

"What is it?" I ask him.

"Di Pietro is here."

"What? Why?" I ask before turning to Noè. Then I realize the only reason why, "Cristiano is back."

Noè only nods at me, placing his hand firmly on my back. Allen leads us down the narrow stairs and back into the club. Di Pietro waits at the bar. He isn't fully healed yet, but if Cristiano is back, he will want to be at my side and demand retribution for the death of his daughter.

"Where is he?" I ask him at once.

"Taking Bendoni to *Claudia*," Di Pietro says.

"The car is running outside."

The three of us leave, making the short trip to my most popular longue. When we pull up to the club, Luca and Felix wait for us. Other enforcers surround the club, harsh lines across their face. News travels fast when the man who has terrorized us has returned home.

"Clear the club," I order to no one in particular, knowing it will be carried out. Some of them move immediately and I watch as the crowd starts to clear.

"Are you ready?" Noè whispers to me. One of the enforcers passes him and Di Pietro guns.

"Yes."

"You're going to meet my father."

"*Amore mio*, your father doesn't scare me."

"He scares me," Noè admits.

"Who gets to kill him again?" Di Pietro asks us.

"Me," is the answer I give.

"He's your family," Di Pietro points out what I've always told him through the years.

"*Lui è un traditore*." He is a traitor, and all traitors meet the same fate.

CHAPTER 31

Adelaide Bendoni

Once the club is cleared, we all enter. Two chairs wait for Noè and I in the club, and I have another brought for Di Pietro. I face the door and sit and wait. Noè takes my hand, waiting with me. My men surround the room, ready to defend me if Cristiano wants to take a desperate shot. Felix stands behind us, he was there the first night I came to Chicago after my father's and brother's deaths. He's been with me ever since. Di Pietro, to my left, he gave me the means and the confidence to become this, to become a queen.

When the door opens again, three enforcers lead in Cristiano. They don't hold him, they don't confine him, because of the man who walks behind him. I stare at him in confusion, this man was not Noè's father, he is too young. He is taller than my husband, but with the same straight blonde hair. To my right, Noè smiles at the man.

"Elio," he greets from my side, not standing

to greet him. "What brings you to my city?"

The man chuckles and unbuttons his jacket, "Your city has caused quite the stir. Father isn't pleased, brother."

His father didn't come, instead he sent his heir to deal with this. The man before me is Noè's older brother. "My apologies, I mean to kill this *stronzo* before he bothered father with this."

Cristiano's face falls, "This is not your city."

Noè stands and I do as well, my husband shows his wedding band to my cousin. "Marry the queen, inherit the city."

"No, this is supposed to be mine! I am supposed to be the boss here!"

"No, Cristiano, you never deserved Chicago. You have never even been a Sanna. Your mother is *una troia* and you are *un stronzo irlandese*. It was clever sending your half-brothers to my club to kill me, sadly that were unsuccessful. They landed a shot in Di Pietro and beat my husband pretty badly. When we killed them, I assume your real father sought revenge, but that bullet landed in Irene."

"You killed my daughter, *figlio di puttana*," Di Pietro curses.

"What I'm not sure on is why you were killing my warehouse workers," I say next, wanting answers to tell their families before I put down my cousin. Not my cousin, actually. He is not my uncle's son. He is a bastard, a traitor, and a murderer.

Cristiano looks over to Elio, my brother-in-law, for aid. No doubt he assumed this evening would go differently. He didn't expect me to marry Noè, he didn't expect me to let a man provide for me and protect me. Elio simply smiles at the man, waiting for him to answer my question. His smile reminds me of my husband.

"I'd answer the lady," he recommends Cristiano.

"I didn't kill your warehouse workers," he says with a cocky smile.

"But you know who did?"

"The rat you let fester started to chew, chew away at your operation. You trusted him, and it served me well."

"Who?"

"He's in the room. You let him into your warehouses. You let him be a spy for you," Cristiano mocks me. I furrow my brow at him. *Spy?* I have few spies. I have some police in my pocket, but they don't know the operation. We keep them in the dark about most things so they can keep their integrity.

I look over the faces of all the men in the room. He knows it's one of them, or he lied and is doing this to torture me. To make me second guess all of their loyalty. They too, are looking at each other, trying to guess who I've had as a spy and who would work against me.

"You are a stupid girl," Cristiano accuses me.

"Don't speak to her that way," Noè demands.

"I did so much for you, Adelaide, and you

betrayed me. I was there for Angelo when your mother died. I made sure the police didn't look into his death, or your fathers. All I wanted was your respect and compliance. I'd have married you off to Noè Bendoni, if that's what you wanted. This could have all been avoided if you'd just had done what I told you and let me have Chicago. Irene could be alive now, if you would have done what you were told."

"Stop it," Noè tells him, and I stop my search though the room. I glance one final time at a face that is staring directly at me. He's not searching like the others.

"You're right, Cristiano. It could have been easier," I look at my supposed cousin again. "I could have given it over to you and let you tell me where to live and who to marry. Maybe it would have been Noè, maybe it would have been someone else. I could have stood behind you and supported your claim to Chicago, but then I wouldn't have been true to my heritage. The Sanna name may die with you, because their blood will live on thought me.

"These men, they would have never been loyal to you, I have had one rat in three years. You had a rat the first day because when I asked if they'd follow you, the men said no. I don't know how you got the rat to follow you, but he will die a traitor like you." I give one look to Luca and nod. He steps forewords, past Elio and to Cristiano. Felix joins him, and when each grab his shoulder they force him onto his knees in front of me. I summon another enforcer, Timothy, to my side and make him take Felix's spot holding down Cristiano.

With a curling finger, Felix comes to my side, I whisper to him, "Raoul Titone." As Felix steps away from me, a shot rings through the air. I hiss and react immediately to the pain in my arm. Enforcers around my rat jump to him, forcing the young man onto his stomach.

"Addy," Noè pulls me into his chest, putting his back to the man that hurt me. I take inventory, the pain is fleeting. I check my left arm and see that the bullet only grazed me.

"I'm fine, I'm fine," I repeat to him over and over again. I take the gun from his waste and pull back from his chest. As I caress his cheek, soothing the panic in his gaze, I add, "A scratch."

He takes a strangled breath, "Addy?"

"Less than what I'm about to give him."

I walk across the room, cocking the gun. Luca smiles at me as I approach Cristiano. "*Arrivederci*, Cristiano." I pull the trigger and Cristiano's blood spatters. Luca and Timothy let him fall to the ground. Noè takes the gun back from me, kissing my forehead, and going to kill Raoul. Four enforcers hold him down, but Noè shoos them off while he takes the kill.

Elio comes up to my side. He hands me his handkerchief to hold over my arm and I take it gratefully. "Not what I expected to happen when he dragged me here, but happy I got to witness it. Welcome to the family, Adelaide."

"Welcome to Chicago, Elio."

CHAPTER 32

Noè Bendoni

A doctor meets us at the house to stitch up my wife. He tends to her in our bedroom while I pour my brother and I something to drink. He sinks into the chair of our parlor, swirling the amber liquid in his glass and smiling at me. I sat across from him, both of us sizing up the other. We were close, as I was raised to be his second. Yet here I am, a re by the right of my wife. Not his equal, no, he is a first son and I'm a second son. But heading Chicago brought me a step closer.

"You married her, I knew you would."

"How angry is Father?"

"When Cristiano burst into his office and remanded recourse, he was pretty pissed. There was a rumor you two married, which is why he sent me. Plus, he is dealing with a lot right now. Canonici is ill, his sons are bickering."

"Will he go to *Italia*?"

"Most likely." My brother took a heavy drink then, knowing that he will likely have to accompany Father to *Italia*. He never enjoyed those particular trips. "I apologize, but I didn't bring you a wedding gift."

I can't help but chuckle. "It was a very quick affair."

"You care for her?"

My smile drops. "Father cannot know."

"He won't hear it from me. In May though, you will both need to be less obvious."

Love is a weakness, one that Father never tolerates. I don't want to imagine what he would put us though if he discovered how deep our bond runs. He doesn't love mother, and never really loved us. We are tools, heirs, enforcers, and nothing more to him.

"I will remember that."

"She is a lovely wife, I am jealous."

"When will you tie the knot with your *promessa*?"

Elio goes cold at the mention of his affianced. "When she is ready." My future sister-in-law is Canonici's only daughter. A fine prize that many covet but is my brother's by all rights and traditions. The two have been engaged since Elio was ten.

We sit in silence for a few more minutes before footsteps sound down the stairs. Addy sees out the doctor before being properly introduced to my brother. We spend the night chatting, laughing, and Elio shares as many childhood stories about me as he can remember. We eat dinner as a family, and Addy shows Elio to his room. She gave him the Master bedroom, no doubt she prepared as if my father was coming, not my brother.

That night, I hold my wife closer, knowing that Cristiano is dead, and the rat is discovered.

EPILOGUE

In May, we go to New York. I meet the whole of the Bendoni family. My father and mother-in-law, some of his cousins. Noè reminds me we must be careful around them. Not like we were around Elio. In New York, we cannot love each other. There are no forehead kisses, no hand holding, and no longing glances. It is almost torture to pretend I do not love my husband.

What we lacked during the day, we made up for at night. Whenever we got behind our bedroom door, Noè and I were attached. We would hold each other, kiss each other, and find pleasure together each night we spent there.

Life returned to normal when we got back from New York. We found a new routine where I managed the longues still, but Noè found use in many parts of the organization. He learned every part of our operation, even visiting some of our suppliers downstate.

Summer ends and on the first cold day of fall

we bury Nonno. He died late at night, asleep in his bed. He's with Nonna now, buried in the cemetery next to her and my parents. Angelo is next to them as well. Noè stays with me to watch all the dirt cover his casket, holding my hand as the leaves turn on a nearby oak.

"I'm sorry he's gone. I'm sorry you don't have any family left."

I smile to myself, "I have you."

"Blood is different." I nod, agreeing with him. Blood is different, but I chose Noè for my family. We go home together and have a luncheon with the many men within the mafia. Di Pietro and Mrs. Di Pietro are there with their many children. Doriano left Chicago not long after Cristiano died, moved to Detroit for a fresh start. He works in the dockyards there now, last I heard.

Di Pietro takes me to the backyard as the luncheon starts to come to a close. We sit at the porch table and look at the roses my mother planted when she was still alive. "You're different now than you were when your father died."

"I didn't know my father well, you know that. I took care of Nonno for three years. It is hurting me more, losing him."

"Will you be alright?"

"I've seen many deaths this year, Di Pietro. I almost lost you, I lost Irene, I killed Cristiano, and Titone's son." I know the last two deserved it. When Noè killed Raoul in the spring, a few other rats ran that had helped him in his plots.

I'd trusted him when I thought Renzi was disloyal, but I put my eggs in the wrong basket. It cost men their lives, that mistake I made, and I'll live with that for the rest of my life. "Nonno was ready to go. He was ready to go home. God has him now, he's with Nonna and his sons."

"The Sanna name is dead."

"Long live the Bendoni's." Di Pietro laughs at me, and I can't contain my smile. I decide then that I want him to be the first to know. Di Pietro has given me so much, he has raised me as his own the three years I have ruled over Chicago. I trust him more than I trust any man. Except maybe my husband.

"The name is dead, but our blood lives on. It continues." I rest my hand on his hand, giving him a small smile.

"Adelaide?"

"A legacy, my legacy."

"Does he know yet?"

I shake my head. "I'm going to tell him tonight," I assure him. "But I wanted you to know."

"Thank you for telling me. How far are you?"

"The midwife thinks about two months, maybe three." I went to my doctor last week, and he recommended me to a midwife that serves many of the mafia wives. She gave me the estimate on my timeline based on my cycle and a short physical examination.

"Congratulations, I am very happy for you. It is time this house had a child in it again."

"Thank you, for everything you've done for me."

"We are not blood, but you are my family, Adelaide."

"And you are mine, Di Pietro." He hugs me before we go back into the house.

Later that night, as Noè holds me tight in his arms, our naked bodies pressing together. His finger run up and down my arm, the one that still bears a scar from the bullet graze that the rat gave me. I turn to face him and place a small kiss on his chest.

"I love you. You know that right."

"I know," he says with a yawn. "I love you too, *mia regina.*"

"But you're right, blood is different. I'm not alone thought, and neither are you."

"We have each other, I know, *amore.*" His eyes closer as he relaxes into the bed, not fully listening to me.

"Our family is growing, Noè," I tell him finally. His beautiful brown eyes shoot open, and he sits up, fully awake.

"Addy?"

I take his hand and place it over my still flat stomach. "*Un principe o una principessa per te, mio re.*"

He gathers me in his arm, kissing my lips and cheek and nose and forehead. Kissing all around my face in joy. My husband pulls me into his lap and cradles me against his chest. "Thank you for choosing me, *reginetta.* Thank you for making me your king and making me a father."

"There was no choice but you."

ACKNOLEDGMENTS

Thank you so much
for reading!

Without amazing readers, there is no author. You are truly why I do this. It is through your support that I continue to write and tell stories.

Of course, a special thank you to the creatures I love most in the world, my horse Claire and two dogs Cooper and Dave. They are the loves of my life and the banes of my existance.

Also, to my friends who are tired of hearing me talk about my stories, here you go, you can finally read them yourselves. To Loren and Ashley for never letting me give up and to Natalia and Olivia who always push me to finish the darn book.

Love you all!

-J.C.D

www.ingramcontent.com/pod-product-compliance
Lightning Source LLC
Chambersburg PA
CBHW071431260626

47170CB00008B/2677